THOU SHALT NOT KILT

THOU SHALT NOT KILT

Liam Ashe

KNAVE

Thou Shalt Not Kilt

www.liamashe.com

First Printing, March 2020

ISBN 978-1-7346854-0-4

Knave Publishing
821 Herndon Ave #141226
Orlando, FL 32803

www.knavepublishing.com

For my parents who
taught me the importance
of the written word

ROAN ISLAND & ALDERMIRE

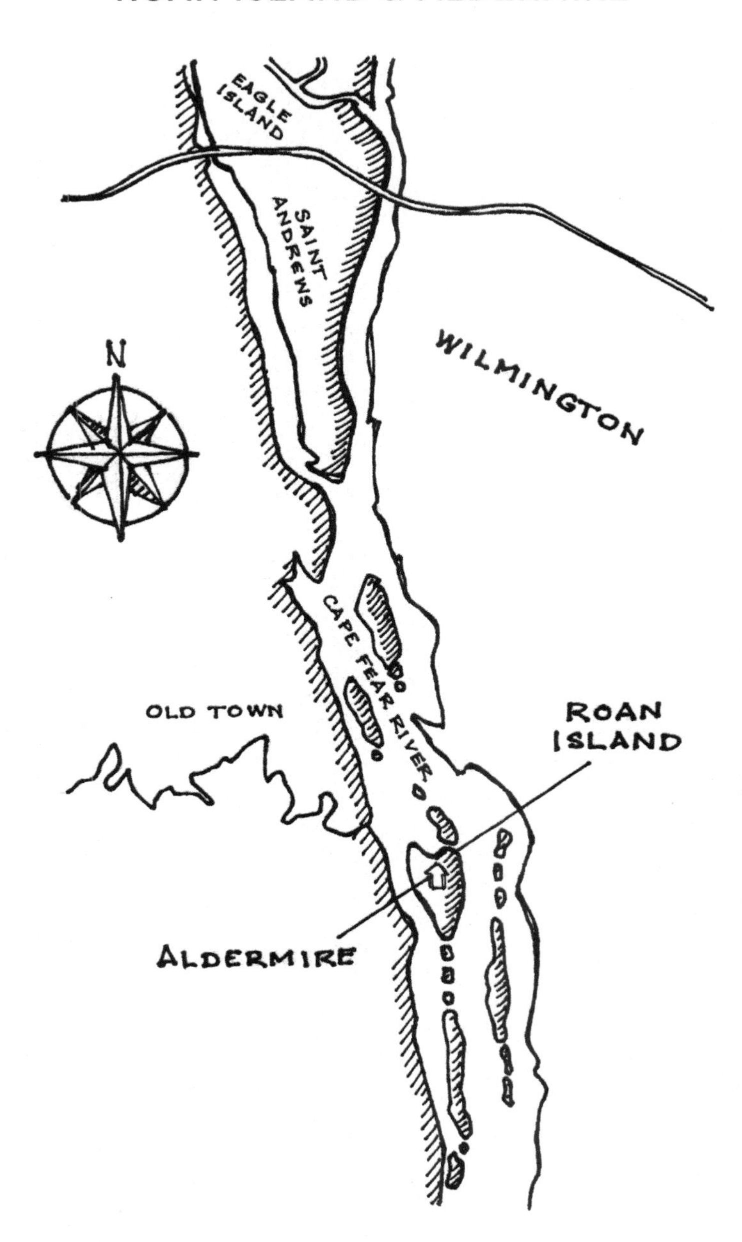

1

Resentment is like drinking poison and waiting for the other person to die.

— Saint Augustine

The last scant rays of afternoon sunlight bathed the cottage bedroom in an amber warmth. For a third time, Elle considered her reflection in the oversized vanity mirror, readjusting the tartan shawl around her shoulders. Beneath the wrap, her sheer charcoal cocktail dress was a piece of borrowed luxury.

One sister's cast-offs are another sister's treasures, she thought. *Still, a little too dark and dreary. Needs a pop.*

From a silver-footed vase of bluebells and thistles, she plucked a sprig of tiny snowflake flowers. She unhooked the antique silver brooch that secured the shawl and repinned the blossoms and woolen cloth in place. The delicate spray of white blooms contrasted the cardinal reds and somber blacks of the Cunningham family tartan, complementing the pale white skin of her neck and face.

"White heather for good luck," she whispered. "God knows I'm gonna need it."

An upswept halo of curls in Elle's favorite shade of honey-kissed burgundy wreathed her face. She evaluated the almost-too-red-to-be-natural color and smiled, turning her head side to side. *Not too bad for a two-week-old home job on a tight budget,* she admitted to herself.

Tucked behind the vase she found one earring, the first of two antique sterling teardrops picked up for a steal in Wilmington. Elle's limited knowledge of Scottish hallmarks suggested the intricately carved pair was from an Edinburgh foundry, likely mid-nineteenth century. They were one of the few luxuries she had allowed herself since the divorce.

A cursory search of the vanity top failed to turn up the second earring. One silver teardrop in hand, Elle took a deep breath, exhaled and scanned the rest of the tiny guesthouse. Every flat surface in her temporary room was camouflaged in research notes, old manuscripts, leather-bound books and discarded clothing.

Elle stepped with care between two rough stacks of sooty, graphite-covered tracing papers—three weeks' worth of grave rubbings. As she navigated the narrow path, her foot found an empty space between marker impressions for Eachann Cameron MacUspaig, born 1747, and Beitiris Kerr MacUspaig, born 1765.

Both interred in the MacUspaig mausoleum on Roan Island, the pair shared a sordid history that Elle knew by line and verse. Beitiris, as Elle recalled, was the second wife of Bearnard, Eachann's third brother. The specific details had been obscured over the intervening 250 years, but family letters suggested the beguiling Beitiris was the center of an epic extramarital scandal.

Elle shook her head. "Some things never change," she murmured with only the slightest hint of a smirk.

Her footing secure, Elle reached for the largest pile of notes on the nightstand. She lifted and fanned through the pages with no trace of the missing earring. She moved methodically from stack to stack, the fading light through the window making the search no easier.

To her surprise, Elle uncovered the teardrop with little fuss, slipped just behind her personal copy of John Stewart's 1880 history of the Stewarts of Appin. She hoped the fleeting sense of satisfaction would continue through the evening ahead.

"Heather, you're already bringing me luck," she said aloud, if only to reassure herself.

Elle closed the cottage door and stepped out into the cool, pine-scented evening air. The last sounds of the blue jays and meadowlarks welcomed her as the setting sun crested over Old Town to the distant west. The failing daylight trimmed the silver expanse of the Cape Fear River with traces of gold and fire.

"Mother nature saves her best for North Carolina in spring." Her mama's words percolated through her mind, mixing with the native sights, sounds and aromas of the island. The familiar sensations of her childhood brought a measure of comfort, even as darkness fell.

Out of habit, she double-checked the door on her temporary home, then the door on its adjacent twin. Elle felt the pair, known on Roan Island as simply the red cottage and the white cottage, were accurately, if unimaginatively, named.

While she took slow, deliberate steps across the estate grounds, the winds of an approaching storm rustled through the leafy alder tree branches overhead. It was only a few hundred feet, but Elle was in no rush to be first at dinner. As she approached the manor house, the breeze carried the baleful, harmonizing notes of a bagpipe from somewhere across the lawn. Though perhaps *harmonizing* was a bit of an overstatement.

Lyle doesn't know when to quit, she thought with an unguarded roll of her eyes. For nearly 500 years the Scots had mastered the intricate, haunting music of the bagpipe; the instrument was as unmistakably Scottish as whiskey, kilts and haggis. With less than a year of practice, she acquiesced, Lyle MacUspaig had squandered several generations of that goodwill. But at least he was trying.

She imagined she could just make out Lyle's silhouette on Aldermire's rooftop patio. As he plodded through a workmanlike verse of "Scotland the Brave," Elle meandered through the cultivated beds of Sweet Betsy, mountain laurel and dwarf crested iris. One of the island's few attractions, the extensive gardens blended traditional Carolina greenery with more exotic flora imported from the MacUspaig's ancestral county in Scotland. For Elle, the flowering trees and shrubs were an excuse to take the longest route from cottage to castle.

Too soon, she approached the wide stone expanse of the estate's grand west terrace. Paved with the same native North Carolina granite that covered the manor house proper, the patio offered Elle a few final moments of peace.

Through the wide French doors, she recognized most of the MacUspaig clan and a few unfamiliar faces already congregated ahead of dinner. The generous cocktail glasses scattered around the library had done little to ease the tense expressions on their faces.

Elle contemplated whether she would be better off with Lyle's bagpipes. Her mind flipped through a weak list of convenient, if not very convincing, excuses. None seemed particularly promising.

As she focused her nerve, Lyle's pipes fell silent and a sharp, bestial howl split the darkness. From his chained perch next to the servants' door, Angus regarded her intrusion of his turf with equal parts suspicion and bravado.

I'm gonna kill that hound, she thought, only half joking.

The gathered guests turned in unison to the arched windows overlooking the patio. On cue, the automatic security lamps sensed Elle's arrival and bathed her in a sudden, brilliant wash of artificial light. She was trapped.

"Damn."

Stealth no longer an option, Elle crossed the patio to the only pair of open French doors. Centered in the doorway, a figure in full kilt and jacket stared into the night. At seventy-eight, aging patriarch Hendry MacUspaig still cut a striking silhouette against the bright lights of the library. A natural athlete like his sons, he had broad shoulders just beginning to lose their decades-long battle against gravity. His thatch of red hair had long since grayed, and the tan undertones had faded from his ruddy complexion.

As the years had passed, Elle thought, Hendry now resembled the home he had once lorded over—gray, granite and beginning to crumble.

"Good evening, Hendry." Elle offered the barest of greetings as she tried to navigate around the figure separating her from the warmth and security of the manor house.

The old man neither replied nor looked in her direction. His dark brown eyes, hooded with exaggerated brows, continued a survey of the trees and gardens from his solitary perch. Undaunted by the slight, Elle stood her ground, making it clear she wouldn't pass her host's father without a response.

After an intentional delay, he turned to give her an unwelcome acknowledgment. "Elspeth."

"You are as charming as ever, Hendry."

"And you, Elspeth Cunningham, are a drunkard, a whore and an embarrassment," he replied without pause. While his frame may have surrendered a bit over the years, his voice hadn't lost its gravel or vinegar.

Elle forced a smile, counting to ten on the fingers now clenched into fists. She held his gaze and let the silence speak for her.

"Stuart was a fool to welcome you into our home," he continued. "But my son has always had a weakness for vile women like yourself."

Elle felt her grimace relax into a natural grin as she looked into the room. "Weakness? Stuart is the only MacUspaig I know who can handle a strong woman as well as a strong whiskey."

"'Yet consider now, whether women are not quite past sense and reason, when they want to rule over men,'" Hendry quoted, returning his eyes to the darkening night.

"Again with the John Calvin?" Elle replied as she stepped around him and into the library. "Hendry, you need to modernize your views. And your references."

A flurry of words to Elle's left caught her attention as a soft hand gripped her wrist.

"Hendry," the sugary voice implored, "I just need to borrow Elle for a second. I hope you don't mind."

Without waiting for the reply that wouldn't come, the hand pulled Elle from Hendry's earshot and farther into the room of clinking glasses and hushed conversations. Caroline Mac Uspaig offered Elle a sincere apology, her Southern lilt giving the words a silvery hint of saccharine.

"I hoped you wouldn't mind," she said. "He's in a rare form, even for Hendry."

The wife of Lyle MacUspaig, Hendry's youngest son, Caroline reminded Elle of the pampered Southern girls who ignored her in college. Not a day over twenty-eight, the younger Mrs. MacUspaig had a wide smile, heavily accented eyes and mop of blond curls that suggested lackadaisical, but only with a significant amount of effort. The belted jumpsuit she had chosen for the evening was, no doubt, too casual for Hendry's liking, but it served to accent her body's curves.

"Actually, it's the warmest welcome that I've gotten from him since I arrived," Elle replied.

"So, what did you get tonight?"

"Let's see, I am a whore, a drunk and an embarrassment."

"I got, oh, what was it?" Caroline gave an exaggerated wrinkle of her brow. "Oh, yes. I am a tramp, a harlot and a gold digger."

"Hellfire, brimstone and cocktails—sounds like a party," Elle said. "Did you point out that tramp and harlot are pretty much the same thing?"

"I didn't have the nerve. And it's nothing more than words. Honestly, I don't think his heart is in it tonight. He seems a million miles away."

"Which is exactly where I'd like him to be," Elle replied in a stage whisper. The two women laughed as they surveyed the room.

Around the library's grand fireplace, four guests, none of whom Elle recognized, posed with Megan, Stuart MacUspaig's current wife and reluctant lady of the manor. Elle found it an awkward scene as their conversation lurched and fell at random measures. Even across the room, she sensed the interaction was forced. They were all waiting for *something*. No one, however, seemed quite sure what they were waiting for.

"Elle, I'm a little surprised to see you. I wasn't sure you'd come. And I love that dress; you look like a million dollars."

Elle ignored the compliment. "Stuart made it clear he wanted me to be here," she replied. "It's the first time I've heard from him since I arrived. I figured it must be important."

Although the two women could not have been more different, Elle suspected Caroline had sensed in her the heart of another outsider on Roan Island. The young woman had inserted herself into Elle's work more than once since her arrival at Aldermire. It was an effort that despite their differences, Elle begrudgingly welcomed.

"Any idea what's up?"

"None at all." Caroline shrugged and nodded to the group camped out at the fireplace. "I'm guessing they don't know, and Lyle swears he doesn't know either. He and Stuart have been at each other all week. I swear they can be worse than children."

Caroline returned her eyes to the larger group and offered to make introductions, but Elle declined.

"I want to say hello to Leith," she replied. "We have some notes to compare before I get in too deep with this new crowd."

"You won't be missing much," Caroline said with a smirk. "And when you two take a break from the graveyard shift, promise me we can do a day in Wilmington or Saint Andrews. You know, 'all work and no play...'"

"After the past couple of months, being a dull girl isn't so bad."

"Promise me anyway. Anything to get me off this island for a bit."

Before Elle could answer, a warm, gentle voice spoke behind her.

"Now Caroline, don't think that I can spare Elle, even for a minute." Leith Daleroch gave both women an abbreviated hug, ending their conversation. As Caroline MacUspaig departed for the well-stocked bar, the small, solid man with an engaging smile took Elle by the arm and guided her to the quiet security of two overstuffed chairs by the library's furthermost bay window.

As he settled her into a worn-leather refuge, Leith gave Elle a tired yet genuine grin. Like Hendry MacUspaig, he was a man in his seventies. According to the local ladies, Leith enjoyed a reputation as quite the charmer in his day. Although he was more than thirty years her senior, his quick wit, bright blue eyes, and cropped white hair still lent him a boyish, irresistible charisma.

Leith unbuttoned his waistcoat, gathered his kilt and took the seat across from Elle. He shook his head and glanced around the room. Following his eye, she again regarded the small party at the fireplace. The two men were bekilted with full jackets and sporrans, and the women wore matching cocktail dress attire. Elle was glad she had taken a few more minutes to polish her look.

The two couples talking to Megan MacUspaig (Elle assumed they *were* couples) were of similar stock and vintage. The pair on the left was clad in the colorful, unmistakable tartan of Clan Buchanan. The woman, who Elle estimated to be in her early sixties, had a regal, confident bearing. Beautiful steel-gray hair provided a neutral frame that highlighted the blue of her eyes. Without effort, she was the center of the conversation, and she knew it. The man Elle guessed to be her husband was little more than an accessory.

She estimated the other two guests to be in their early to mid-sixties. They were a lively pair dressed in a coordinating kilt and skirt of MacFarlane Dress, although the woman wore a shawl of either Hunting Stewart or perhaps MacLeod of Harris. Each holding a nearly empty whiskey tumbler, the two nodded and laughed on cue as the Clan Buchanan woman held audience.

"It's such a pleasure to have you dining with us tonight." Leith's words snapped Elle back to the conversation. "Angus was kind enough to let us know that you had arrived. Legend has it that basset hound's yowl could empty the MacUspaig crypt."

Elle smiled at the attempted humor before turning back to the group across the room.

"I wasn't expecting anyone from off-island," she said. "Quite the party."

"Neither was I. Still, we haven't quite managed a celebratory atmosphere, I'm afraid."

Elle nodded without thinking. Sensing the emotional chill in the room, she pulled her wrap a bit tighter around her shoulders.

"Elle, my dear," he continued, "that scarf may have tendered some warmth against the night air, but I'm afraid it won't offer much comfort in here."

"Aldermire has never been particularly warm to outsiders, but tonight seems worse than usual," she agreed. "I had plans to take the ferry over to Saint Andrews for a dinner with friends. Well, until Stuart asked me to stay on Roan tonight. He hasn't spoken two words to me since I've been here and suddenly, I'm on the VIP list. I have no idea why, but I've been dreading this all afternoon."

"My dear, as you know, the mood at Aldermire has been, let's say, MacBethish for some time now," Leith offered. "All hurly-burly and battles lost and won."

"So what's different about tonight? And, for that matter, why the last-minute dinner?" she asked. "Caroline swears she and Lyle are out of the loop."

Leith rubbed his hands together and looked to the fire. "In life, when issues are left unresolved, pressure builds. As humans, we crave closure. Loose ends are distractions that wear away at even the most resolute of men. And, of course, women."

"Very true," Elle offered without understanding his point. She hoped her words would encourage him to follow with something more substantial.

"When that pressure reaches a tipping point, we are called to action," Leith continued. "Tonight, my dear, is one of life's tipping points. This family cannot continue as it is, and decisive action is required."

Unsure how to respond, Elle settled for a quizzical look.

"I can't say any more," Leith said with a somber shake of his head. "But you won't be held in suspense any longer than necessary. All will be explained tonight at dinner. Stuart has..."

Leith's words trailed off as a pair of robust voices echoed from the entry hall. As the conversation grew louder, the brothers MacUspaig entered the library and greeted the guests. Clearly, Elle thought, the two were at odds. She knew this was nothing unusual, although this time, Lyle's scowl suggested that his older brother held the upper hand. As the pair made their way around the room, Leith stood and offered Elle a drink.

"I appreciate the offer," Elle said, "but I'm swearing off the spirits for a bit."

"My dear, I am very sorry," he said with a concerned furrow of his brow. "I didn't mean to dangle temptation in front of you like that."

"No worries. And I don't have a problem with drinking," Elle said with a smile. "In fact, I'm quite good at it. The problem is usually after I've been drinking."

The old man chuckled. "I think it was Richard Brinsley Sheridan who said, 'A bumper of good liquor will end a contest quicker than justice, judge, or vicar.'"

Elle laughed despite herself. "Was that from *The Duenna* or *The School for Scandal*?"

"My dear, you remain a wellspring of surprises," he said, the spark returning to eyes. "I didn't know your literary interests crossed the North Channel."

"Irish playwrights aren't a personal passion, but it comes with the academic territory."

"Delightful!" He laughed and turned toward the bar. "Honestly, I'm not sure where Sheridan buried that bon mot. It's just something my own father used to say while sampling good scotch. And, to my father, all scotch was good scotch."

"Well, I appreciate the offer, but tonight I think I'd better stay on my toes."

"As you wish, my dear." Over his shoulder as he made his way across the room, he added, "Still much to discuss. Save my seat!"

Unattended and exposed, Elle pressed herself deep into the overstuffed gentleman's chair. With luck she could evade further conversations and bide her time until dinner. Her efforts were unsuccessful as Megan MacUspaig, lady of the house and Elle's hostess, crossed from the fireplace to the kitchen. Her path brought her within arm's reach of Elle's hiding place.

As she passed, Megan gave her guest a brief yet naked glare. Despite her natural instinct to retaliate, Elle took the look as it was intended, a warning shot sent straight across her bow. She was now sailing through hostile waters and had been put on notice by the local armada: proceed with extreme caution.

In the nearly thirty years since she first met Megan Mac Uspaig, previously Megan Bloom, Elle had enjoyed little face-to-face interaction with her contemporary. Tall and naturally athletic with dark hair and piercing gray eyes, Megan gave the distinct impression of one who shouldn't be crossed. Elle was all too happy to oblige.

What little she knew of Stuart's wife Elle could sum up in three simple observations. First, she was strong. Her ironclad interior was a well-suited match for her imposing exterior. Second, she was smart. Megan rarely came across as well-educated, but her eyes hinted at the sharp, calculating intelligence within. Finally, Megan was a survivor. Elle was familiar with many of the tales told of the colorful Bloom family, and her bet was on Megan to outlast them all.

As his wife disappeared into the kitchen, Stuart Mac Uspaig materialized at Elle's side. Fresh from a win against his younger brother, the lord of Aldermire had a cocky glow about him that well suited his careless charm and, Elle would admit, roguish good looks.

Uninvited, he co-opted Leith's chair, blocking her exit and monopolizing her view of the room. "So, you do exist," he joked without introduction.

Elle bristled at being caught so easily off her guard; she should have expected this. Stuart had a history of slipping beneath her radar. A trademark sharp retort nearly tripped past her lips.

You need this money, she reminded herself. *Hell, you need a home.* For a few moments, she weighed her alternative approaches from challenging to charming. Elle opted for charming.

"So, so very busy," she said with weak smile. "I'm six weeks into the grant period and just getting my feet wet with primary research. You MacUspaigs are a fascinating bunch. So much to learn, so little time." She winced, which did little to improve her smile.

"Six weeks at Aldermire, and I've seen you, what? Twice?" he countered. "I blame Leith. He's been monopolizing your time, he and all the other ghosts that haunt these miserable halls. I had no idea you prefer the company of the soon-to-be-dead over me."

"They can be so much warmer," Elle replied in measured tones. "Older generations like Leith and your father are living, breathing history. In my field, they are worth an entire shelf of books. When they die, decades of family history, all in the first person, die with them." She hoped she was still charming or, at the very least, earnest and academic.

"So, all those family histories really keeping you warm at night?" he asked with a hushed, guttural tone. "That's one thing I know I can do better."

"That didn't work out so great for me last time, and this go around you're married," she countered. "I've made my share of mistakes and, occasionally, I learn from it. It's cliché, but you and I are nothing but ancient history." If her words registered, Stuart refused to let on.

"Elle, I thought you liked ancient history," he said.

"Ancient," Elle repeated with a grimace. For a moment she regarded Stuart through the hazy lens of the past. At forty-six, he had reached a plateau where his strong features perfectly complemented the maturity of a man in his prime. His dark brown hair was tinged with silver above the temples, and the weathered lines of his face granted him a welcome gravitas.

Like many former Highland athletes, he was tall and broad. He had a surety and grace of movement that belied his imposing frame. For more than two decades, he had been lord and master of Aldermire, and Elle admitted it finally suited him.

"So how about we relive a little of that history?" Stuart continued. "I can drop by the cottage after dinner. We have some catching up to do."

His easy charm never skipped a beat. He held her gaze for a split second longer than she found comfortable. Elle was acutely aware that Stuart was in her space and, damn it, he knew how to leverage that closeness to his advantage. For the second time in one evening, Elle was trapped.

"Stuart, my boy, would you begrudge an old man his favorite chair?" Leith asked, as though from nowhere. He appeared at Stuart's side, a generous tumbler of whiskey in his firm grasp. Elle hadn't noticed him approach, and she had no idea how long he had been hovering. Regardless, she welcomed the interruption.

Stuart continued to hold Elle's gaze. "Certainly not," he said. "But I think Megan may be ready for us in the dining room."

Leith laughed, which broke the undercurrent of tension. "Well, then. No sense wasting good whiskey," he chortled. With an exaggerated toast to no one in particular, he raised his glass and downed the thick amber liquor in one quick drought.

"Shall we?" the old man offered, and Elle accepted his proffered hand with relief.

"Elle," Stuart continued, undeterred, "let's finish catching up after dinner. I'd love to hear about everything you've uncovered so far at Aldermire."

"Ah, Stuart, so many stories to tell!" Leith chimed in with a doddering lilt. "I could go on for hours." Turning to the younger MacUspaig, he reiterated, "Hours..."

Sly dog, Elle thought, squeezing the older man's hand for running interference. *Dinner is looking up.*

2

Through treachery, bad luck or natural selection, a number of Scottish family names have come to an end during the twentieth and twenty-first centuries. According to electoral records, and despite the Scottish tradition of spellings changing nearly every generation, several clans are noted to be nearing extinction.

Some, like the MacCaas and the MacQuoids, may be related to current thriving families, in both cases to the modern clan of Mackay. Others, like Clan Mc Ilhagga, Clan Loghty and Clan Daleroch are distinct branches that may soon be pruned from the Scottish family tree due to a simple lack of viable bloodlines.

Clan MacUspaig, for example, has its roots in Hebridean tradition, derived from the Gaelic version of a Norse family name. Although the clan died out in Scotland in the early twentieth century, a single family line has been traced to the eastern Carolina coast of the United States, where the clan has ebbed and waned for nearly 200 years.

— Elspeth Cunningham Mackay,
The Extinct Clans of Old Scotland

Dinner was, for Aldermire, an informal affair. Through luck or divine intervention, Elle found herself seated between Leith on her left and the steel-coifed woman on her right. The arrangement ensured ample distance between herself and the lord and lady of Aldermire.

Heather, keep working your magic, Elle thought with a smile.

More than a dozen silver chafing dishes offered an embarrassment of warmed entrees, seasonal vegetables and cold salads. Despite the obvious bounty, Megan MacUspaig made a point of apologizing at regular intervals throughout the meal.

"Stuart asked that I send Lainie into town for the evening," she repeated more than once. "This is all I could pull together on my own."

"On her own?" Leith whispered to Elle. "Not bloody likely."

The dishes, to the last dessert, were specialties of Lainie Daleroch, Aldermire's resident housekeeper and Leith Daleroch's youngest daughter. Although no formal introductions were made, Elle's other dinner companion wasted no time initiating a conversation.

"Dr. Coira MacLain Buchanan-Berman," she offered with a practiced rhythm. "An absolute pleasure to meet you, Ms. Mackay. Leith has told me so much about the work you're doing at Aldermire. There are few things so precious and worth preserving as our shared Scottish heritage. I applaud your worthwhile endeavors."

"So very nice to meet you, Dr. Buchanan-Berman," Elle replied. "I don't think I've..."

"Please, only my clients call me Dr. Buchanan-Berman. Coira is fine," she interjected. "Do you mind if I call you Elle? I don't see a ring so I'm assuming Mackay is your family name."

"Actually," Elle said, "I'm divorced, but I..."

"When I was in Durham at school, I met the most charming young man," Coira continued without a breath. "Edward Mackay was his name, if I recall correctly. This was years before I met my husband, Allen." She acknowledged Allen, seated beside her, with a slight nod over her shoulder. He leaned forward in an attempt to introduce himself. He was unsuccessful.

"Edward's family was, I believe, from Durham," she continued. "At least at the time his mother still lived outside of Wake Forest. I must find out if you all are related. Such a small world. Now Leith has told me so much about your work. You must simply eat, drink and breathe history. Elle, have you ever been to Durham? The Nasher Museum is beyond description. Their Hudson School collection is not to be missed. You've never seen an Albert Bierstadt until you've seen it at the Nasher."

Unable to interject, Elle sat back and accepted her fate. Over the next half hour she received a complete masterclass on the life and works of William Hart, Asher B. Durand, Thomas Hill and several others whose names quickly faded from her memory.

Despite the flood of new information, Elle found the arrangement very convenient. "I'm the perfect dinner guest, and I haven't had to say a word," she admitted to Leith later that evening. Between bites of sweet potato biscuit and apple-dressed pork chop, an occasional "Hmmm" or "Really? Fascinating!" was enough to keep her dinner date at full throttle. This left Elle to focus on what she found most important—Lainie's flair for Carolina cuisine.

Following a detailed retelling of Thomas Cole's steamship voyage through the Erie Canal, Coira broke her narrative to refill her plate. Elle noticed that the doctor was partial to the sautéed hominy and salted collard greens. While she considered a second trip to the buffet, Elle opted to stay put and enjoy the silence.

"Quite the talker," Leith commented, again as though from nowhere. "She is certainly a force of nature," he said without any hint of malice. "You look a bit dazed, my dear." His blue eyes sparkled with a fatherly mix of levity and concern.

"She clearly knows her stuff," Elle said, unsure what other compliment to pay her new acquaintance. "I'll never look at a Frederic Edwin Church landscape the same way again. So how does she know the MacUspaigs?"

"Oh, she hadn't gotten there yet?" Leith said with a surprised smile. "Still on the Hudson Valley School, I assume? Dr. Coira MacLain Buchanan-Berman is an old MacUspaig family friend. For the past forty years she's been a fixture on the Wilmington social scene. I have no doubt she knows your mother. And, before you ask, she's a Ph.D., not a medical doctor. Sociology, I believe."

"So why did Dr. Coira MacLain Buchanan-Berman make the invite list this evening?"

"Ah, that's a bit more complicated," Leith replied. "She has been involved with Aldermire for several years in a historical and cultural capacity. I'm being purposefully vague, but you'll probably learn more tonight. I'm surprised she never mentioned her work here."

"We never got that far," Elle said. "We were still on Thomas and his steamship."

"Thomas, eh," Leith responded. "Doughty, Cole, Hill or Moran?"

Elle laughed. "Please don't start," she said with a smile. "So, who is the second couple? I managed to dodge introductions before dinner."

Leith leaned in and looked around the table.

"Well, you've already met Coira and her husband, Allen," he whispered in a conspiratorial tone. He nodded toward the other pair Coira had entertained before dinner. The husband was tall and lanky with the infectious, gregarious nature of a true Scot. His curly red hair and short beard were streaked with a generous wash of gray. The woman matched him perfectly, both in look and personality. Her hair was a softer, richer red, not far from what Elle had tried to achieve with the home kit.

"The tall fellow is Red MacFarlane," he continued. "Red is Hendry's financial advisor. While I manage the legal issues, Red handles the estate money for all three of the MacUspaig men. His wife, Anne, is in something businessy...let's say human resources for the sake of conversation. I adore them both. When Anne can sneak a word past Coira, she is a gifted storyteller. Lived all over the world, you know. Got all that?"

"I won't remember a word," Elle said. "I have never been very good at recalling who is who."

"Not true, my dear," Leith replied. "You have a God-given gift for the smallest of details. Names, dates, places—simply amazing. I've worked with a dozen researchers like you over my career as an amateur historian, but never one with your talent for facts like those."

"You are a charmer," Elle replied with genuine affection. "Well, let's just say I can't remember names when it comes to the living. The dead I never forget."

Their conversation was again interrupted by the voices of the MacUspaig brothers. Standing at the small bar next to the buffet table, the pair was exchanging a second volley of heated words.

"Another convivial evening at Aldermire," Leith said. "Sounds like Lyle is trying to up the stakes. Stuart is maintaining his calm. I suspect he's enjoying this."

Separated by more than twenty years in age, Stuart and Lyle could be mistaken for father and son. They shared the same dark brown hair and the same lantern jaw. Tonight, however, they antagonized one another as only brothers could.

Shorter than his older brother by nearly three inches, Lyle made up for the difference in height and age with fire. His words were difficult to discern over the hushed conversations around the table, but his tone was unmistakable. Lyle's voice contained a hint of threat, and Stuart was egging him on with a sly smile.

Returning to her seat with a generous helping of collard greens and smoked ham, Coira did her best to lighten the mood with a change of subject.

"I have an idea that I've shared with Hendry and Red," she said. "It could be the next step in what we all hope to build here on Roan Island."

Once she was certain she had the full attention of the seated group, she continued. "Our informal programming at Aldermire has really taken root over the past five years. I think this coming January, we should turn the Burns Night dinner into the bedrock of something more. Perhaps a little history, a little culture, a little Scotch. We could make a weekend of it."

Caroline MacUspaig gave a little clap with a broad smile. "That sounds absolutely divine! And it would be a perfect chance to fund some of the improvements we can't afford yet for the cottages and the gardens."

"I know we are still a good nine months out, but it's never too early to get started," Coira continued. "I propose we select an honored clan each year. It will help get the word out and guarantee we fill a few spots. Any ideas for our inaugural year?"

As the table fell quiet, the quarrel between the two brothers again broke the silence. The exchange had elevated past fraternal banter into an angry back and forth.

Megan glanced at her husband over her shoulder, then back to her guests. "I don't know half about what you all do regarding these clans and families," she said. "I do know that Stuart is always going on about all the Gunns that live over in Wilmington. There must be a dozen of them on the mainland."

"Hmm, they are always very well represented at the Eagle Island Highland Games," Coira replied. "And they have their first Chief in more than 230 years. An excellent suggestion, Megan."

Megan blushed, but Elle felt her hostess' attention was still on her husband and brother-in-law. As she studied Megan's expression, she felt there was something wrong. Megan's open hostility was nothing new, and Elle could accept that. Tonight, she imagined, there was a thinly concealed hint of hesitancy, or perhaps regret, to her actions. The lady of the manor was keeping it together, but just barely.

While Coira's husband and both MacFarlanes voiced support for Megan's suggestion, Hendry sat silent. The MacUspaig patriarch had said nothing throughout the meal. He stared, glowering at the family crest hanging above the fireplace.

Caroline MacUspaig raised her hand, her face pinched with an exaggerated sense of concern. "Keep in mind, this is going to be expensive," she warned. "We'll have to fly the Chief and his family over from Scotland. We're looking at several thousand dollars.

"And Elle has the only finished cottage on Roan," she continued. Elle caught the side-eyed glare from Megan. "We'll need to put them up at the Saint Andrew's Inn for at least four or five nights." She shook her head. "The more we spend, the less we make."

"Caroline, please remember that it's not about the money," Coira said. "This would be a purely not-for-profit endeavor. What we do we do for the enrichment of our culture and for the education of our future generations. The money is irrelevant."

Caroline grimaced. "Irrelevant when you have always enough," she muttered under her breath.

Coira ignored her. "Speaking of culture and education, have the rest of you had the delight of meeting Ms. Elle Mackay? She and her work are simply fascinating!"

Elle appreciated the woman's praise. Although she felt that, perhaps, *fascinating* was an overstatement.

"I don't think I had the chance to say one word about my research," she whispered to Leith. "Still, a compliment is a compliment. I'll take it."

"Leith has already introduced each of you to Ms. Mackay, so do say hello to her after dinner," Coira concluded.

"Elle Cunningham Mackay?" Anne MacFarlane asked. "You must be one of Gavina's girls!"

"Yes. I must," Elle replied with a weak smile.

"I've known your mother for probably thirty years," Anne said. "Oh, we've heard so much about you..."

The words hung in the air as the group fell silent. Anne caught herself before asking a follow-up question. The two off-island couples stared at Elle for a second longer than she found comfortable.

With a hearty laugh, Red MacFarlane broke the silence. "Alright, Coira, I'll bite." To Elle he added, "Miss Cunningham Mackay, the good doctor has me intrigued, and I don't want to wait until after dinner. What are you doing here at Aldermire?"

"Yes, Elle. What *do* you do here?" Megan spat, with perhaps a bit more venom than intended. The guests colluded to ignore the gaffe, leaving Elle on the hook to explain her presence.

"By trade, I'm a researcher and author," she replied.

"Oh, how exciting!" Anne said with delight. "A real, published author in our midst. You *must* do a reading after dinner. Have you written anything we may have read?"

Elle shook her head. "Not likely," she conceded. "While I do focus on Scottish history and family ancestries, my work tends to lean more toward the academic. And by academic, I mean dry and dreadfully dull."

Leith, who had been silent for several minutes, offered his support. "Elle, my dear, you're being far too harsh on yourself and the world of academia. Some of our family histories are filled with mystery, intrigue, romance and suspense."

"You just have to skip a few generations here and there to find the good stuff," Elle said. "Sadly, in the interests of accuracy, I have to keep all the boring parts in. History isn't all thrills and chills."

Red nodded his approval. "Is your next book on the Mac Uspaigs and Roan Island? Both share rich, if not always happy, histories."

"Only in part," Elle replied. "The world of academic family research is changing. With globalization, online forums, crowdsourcing, and DNA testing, there's been a recent renaissance in the study of ancestries and family trees. Many of the old clan histories I used to focus on, however, are literally writing themselves. So, right now I'm studying the trees that have been pruned a little too carefully."

Red laughed. "Pruned? How cryptic!" he chided. "So how does that relate to the MacUspaigs?"

"Actually, it's both the MacUspaigs and the Dalerochs," Leith added, nodding to Hendry seated at the far end of the table. "I must admit that genealogical research has always been my secret passion. At a conference last year, Elle and I had the most delightful talk. Neither of us could think of any current work being done to chart and document our Scottish clans that may be facing extinction."

"I had never thought of such a thing," Dr. Buchanan-Berman noted, "until Leith told me about this project. Do continue."

"Well, when we refer to a clan as extinct, it means that the name is no longer in use," Elle said. "Some clan names disappear simply due to poor spelling. For example, the MacKemzys found in references to the seventeenth century Battle of Worcester were likely just MacKimzeys and, even later, the modern-day Kimseys. We no longer see traces of the MacKemzys because their existence was owed to nothing more than lousy record keeping."

"Instead, we are choosing to focus on the clans who have come to the end of a road," Leith continued. "Historic families like Clan MacQuoid and Clan Loghty may have already disappeared. In each case, the last known name bearer has died without a new generation to carry on the torch."

"Many other clans are nearing the verge of extinction," Elle added. "In academic genealogy we call this part of the Galton–Watson process which looks at the rise and fall of family surnames from a statistical perspective. To make a very long story a little shorter, I proposed the project to the Scottish Trust in New York, and they agreed to fund my research."

"So why Aldermire?" Red asked.

"This is a unique situation," Elle said. "First, it's the unlikely home to two such clans. As far as my research suggests, the last of the Dalerochs and the MacUspaigs are all now living on Roan Island. Hendry and Leith are the patriarchs of the final branches of their respective family trees. Second, I had a talented research partner in Leith. His knowledge of both families is extensive. And third, it was the perfect research opportunity since I was already personally familiar with the MacUspaigs."

"*Personally* familiar," Megan repeated.

Leith cut her off. "We've had a most remarkable time. Between the library and the family crypt, Elle and I are up to our necks in the history of both clans."

"The family crypt?" Anne asked. "Sounds terrifying in the most delicious way. What skeletons have you uncovered down among the cobwebs?"

Elle shrugged and said, "Nothing quite that exciting. The crypts are most useful when confirming name spellings, birth dates, death dates—the sort of things we find in old letters or family Bibles. Our forefathers were usually more careful with their facts when carving them in stone."

"What a shame," Anne said with a profound tone of disappointment. "No wooden stakes through rotting corpses or disembodied spirits seeking revenge?"

"Dear God, Anne," Coira said. "I never knew you had such a vivid imagination."

"Our granddaughter is a sullen teen now," Anne replied. "Horror movies seem to be part of this unfortunate stage in her adolescent evolution. Every time I walk through the family room, someone is dying a horrible death on the television. I suppose it's rubbed off a bit."

"Well, I hate to disappoint her, but real crypts are far less exciting than the movies suggest," Elle said. "The hardest part was actually getting the crypt opened. The door hadn't been unlocked in nearly sixty years."

"Since Hendry's mother—Stuart and Lyle's grandmother—died, well before either boy was born," Leith interjected.

"The rooms are somewhat vented to the surface, so we did find several rodent skeletons and two or three raccoon nests," she continued.

"Other than the trinkets, baubles and stray bones the little bandits have collected, the crypts are fully unremarkable," Leith said.

"And let's hope they stay that way," Coira offered as a toast to the dinner guests. A round of clinking wine glasses signaled their collective approval.

During Elle's brief lecture on dying clans, the MacUspaig brothers had moved their argument to the library, out of earshot from the guests. Without either a host or set courses to keep the party progressing in unison toward dessert, dinner was a directionless affair. For over forty minutes, conversations meandered, though Elle felt one question remained unasked, "Does anyone know why we are here?"

She filled the time reviewing her most recent research with Leith. Elle detailed her suspicions regarding the scandalous Beitiris Kerr MacUspaig and her thoughts about the family's connections to a similarly named clan in eighteenth century Edinburgh. Her next task, she noted, would be corralling an imposing stack of original wills, certificates and letters, all of which needed to be transcribed, scanned, cross-referenced and filed. The research had been tedious and, to date, not very rewarding.

"How has your work been faring?" she asked.

"Well, my dear," Leith said, "I finished checking the dates found in the crypt against those in the family records. There were only a few discrepancies, which I have highlighted for your review. I did locate two wall vaults that didn't match any available records. Both were children under the ages of two or three, which may explain why their lives don't appear elsewhere in more detail.

"The loss of a child is so very, very sad," he concluded with a shake of his head.

"Well, that's new information and a good start," Elle said in encouragement. "Any luck with the raccoon collections Anne was so interested in?"

Leith gave a small chuckle. "No, nothing quite as macabre as Anne had hoped," he said. "The three buttons are, in fact, Scottish sterling, as is the little moon pendant. The fabric strips are tattered silk, likely from a memorial wreath placed decades ago.

"While it's not my area of expertise, I was certain the bones are human," he continued. "A friend at the University of Winston-Salem agreed. He suggests they might be from one of the crypts, treasures found first by rats, then by the raccoons. He estimates that they are likely 100 or more years old."

"Damn," Elle said. "Well, the crypt had been worth a look. Nothing at all warranted noting?"

"Well, just one thing I'm looking into," Leith added. "The buttons are hallmarked to a John Eaton in Glasgow, probably around 1820 or 1830. I wish I could determine out of which vault these were pilfered. I don't know that they'd solve a mystery, but they've got me curious."

Their conversation was cut short by the return of Stuart and Lyle MacUspaig. The younger of the two sat next to his wife, his face flush with embarrassment or anger, Elle thought. The older brother set an empty whiskey tumbler on the bar, took his place at one end of the table and tapped his knife against an unused water glass.

"Everyone," Stuart announced to the room. "Thank you all for coming out to Aldermire tonight. I know what you're thinking, or better yet, what you're wondering. You've been patient all evening, so let's just get down to business."

The room fell silent as the guests abandoned their conversations. While most eyes focused on Stuart, Hendry turned to look out the window and across the lawns of Aldermire.

Stuart returned to his feet and made his way slowly around the table. "Tonight, I just wanted dinner with the people most important to me—my family, my trusted advisors and my close friends."

"Wait a goddamned minute," Megan interjected. "Most important? You expressly sent Lainie and my own son off Roan for the evening. So now neither of them is important to you as family?"

Megan shook her head, then bore her gaze down on Stuart. Without looking at Elle, she added, "Then, at the very least, explain to me why *she* is here?" She didn't need to refer to Elle by name. The intent of her words was lost on no one.

"Ah, my dear, direct Megan," Stuart said. "I can always count on you to approach every family gathering with tact and civility." He stopped his pacing behind his young sister-in-law's chair, directly across the table from Elle.

"Why *is* she here?" he repeated. "Elle, and I'm assuming you are referring to Elle, is here tonight by my invitation. As you've all just been reminded, she is chronicling the storied history of Clan MacUspaig. This dinner is the start of a new chapter in that tale. I'd like her to witness this firsthand."

"New chapter?" Red MacFarlane asked with a good-natured guffaw. "Good God, you all are a cryptic bunch tonight."

"Well, no need to sugarcoat this," Stuart said. He moved back to his seat at the head of the table but declined to sit. "I have reached a crossroads in my life, and I've come to realize that my life should, in fact, be about *me*. Not the family, not this rotting estate, not my tactless wife, not our insufferable, shared history. I've spent more than forty-five years chasing after everyone else's whims and demands. That's done."

As Stuart paused to let the words sink in, Lyle's eyes darted between his father and his brother.

"What the hell are you saying?" Lyle demanded. Seated beside him, Caroline reflexively gripped her husband's hand.

"First, little brother, Megan and I are getting a divorce," Stuart answered. The dumbfounded guests turned their attention from their host to the soon-to-be-ex Mrs. MacUspaig.

"You bastard," Megan growled through clenched teeth. Her chest and neck began flushing deep crimson as she struggled to keep her composure. "We had discussed this, but you swore you hadn't made up your mind."

"Consider my mind made up," he countered. To the rest of the table, he said, "And given a few critical legal arrangements we made before marriage, sweet Megan has no claim to Aldermire or what remains of the MacUspaig estate."

Megan buried her face in her hands while the rest of the dinner party looked on in a confused mix of shock and sympathy. Elle had never seen her so vulnerable or so hurt.

After several awkward seconds of silence, Caroline was the first to speak. "Megan," she asked with deep concern in her voice, "does this mean you're leaving Aldermire?"

Before Megan could respond, Stuart gave a harsh laugh. "Actually, Caroline, it means that you all will be leaving Aldermire."

Lyle released his wife's hand and stood, shoving his chair back from the table. "Who the hell do you think you are?" he demanded. The two brothers stood, facing one another in silence. To Elle, the incongruity of Lyle's anger and Stuart's calm was unsettling. It was though the antagonistic game they had played their entire lives was now entering a final round.

"I am the sole owner of this island and everything on it," Stuart said. "There's no secret in that. Father transferred ownership to me after Quacey and I were married, a good two years before you were born, Lyle."

Stuart let those words rest a moment, then addressed the gathered dinner party. "That also means that I am free to sell Aldermire or just level this damn place and develop Roan Island from the ground up. And that's the only decision I have left to make."

The silence cast over the guests was broken as several voices began to interject in urgent concern. The jumble of protests came to a head. Stuart, Elle believed, was enjoying the chaos and discord he had sewn. He had picked one hell of a way to dive into his midlife crisis.

To command the attention of the room, Dr. Buchanan-Berman stood and raised both hands. It worked.

"Stuart, this is simply unacceptable," she announced over the sudden hush. "You know damn well that many of us here have worked for nearly a decade to protect the history of your family and this estate. The programs, the gardens, the events, the fundraising—all of this is to ensure a future for Aldermire. This community is far bigger than you alone, Stuart. We represent several generations of the families who built this region.

We will—and I mean this to my last breath—persevere by any means necessary."

"Coira," Stuart replied with a hint of condescension. "Persevere or not, I don't care. Say what you will and do what you want, but all of you will no longer have a home on Roan Island."

Coira leaned forward and placed both palms flat on the table. "Stuart, I'm surprised by you," she said with a practiced calm. "You grew up in this community. Hell, you were a champion at the Eagle Island Games for more years than I can count. This heritage is part of your history, part of your family's history. Roan Island would be nothing without the MacUspaigs and a dozen other families, and you would be far less a man without each of us."

"Coira, I've known you my entire life, but perhaps you're just getting to know the real me." Stuart again took his seat at the head of the table and folded his arms. The doctor looked to Hendry and then Red MacFarlane. Red shook his head slightly, and she took her seat.

"Stuart, this isn't over," she said with an even conviction.

The guests sat in silence until Caroline implored her husband, "Lyle, he can't do this. This is our home."

"Dad," Lyle repeated, "please tell us he can't do this."

From his seat at the far end of the table, Hendry raised his head. He appeared to Elle as a man on whom the weight of the world had descended. For the first time since dinner began, Hendry spoke.

"Discontent is an ungrateful sin," he spat at his older son. "You have been given everything in this world, Stuart. God has gifted you, and you have returned his benevolence with selfishness and bile. There is no work, however vile or sordid, that does not glisten before God."

His plea unanswered, Lyle turned to Leith. "You're our lawyer, damn it. Do something."

"Stuart and I have been discussing this at great length," Leith said. "I wish I could have broached the subject with you all earlier, but my hands were tied. While this family means the world to me, Stuart *is* my client."

Leith folded his napkin, setting it across his plate. He shook his head. "I've looked at this from every angle. Stuart is the sole, legal owner of both Roan Island and the Aldermire estate. No matter how odious you find his decision, the law is clear. The decision is his and his alone to make."

As Leith's words sank in, there was a final moment of silence. The room erupted as the MacUspaigs and guests fought for attention and answers from their host.

Elle pulled the sprig from beneath her silver pin and dropped it on the table. "I think your luck has run out."

She looked to her left, where Leith's latest tumbler of whiskey sat untouched since Stuart's announcement. As the rest of the guests continued to escalate the conversation, Elle picked up the stubby glass and studied the warm amber liquid. "Why the hell not?" she said and downed the double.

"Gonna be a long night," Elle said to Leith as she made her way from the table and to the bar. "Plus, how much damage can I do on an island?"

3

When it comes to my own turn to lay my weapons down, I shall do so with thankfulness and fatigue, and whatever be my destiny afterward, I shall be glad to lie down with my fathers in honor.

— Robert Louis Stevenson

A shrill, anguished wail flooded the morning air and slipped through the alder trees that surrounded the red cottage. Bundled in her bed tighter than a newborn bairn, Elle resented the intrusion.

"Am I awake?" she asked out loud. Uncertain, she drifted between the real world and an imaginary landscape of rocking chairs and long-tailed cats. A second discordant note—no, more of a dying squeal, Elle thought—snapped her back to her tiny, cluttered bedroom. "Definitely awake."

Several more belabored notes followed. Strung together, they approximated the melody of "Flower of Scotland", or at least an attempt at it.

"Who the hell practices the bagpipes at..." she said as she reached for her nightstand clock. "Christ, seven in the morning?" Despite her protests, the bagpipes continued without mercy.

"Lyle, you're a dead man," she muttered with a grimace.

With considerable effort, Elle was able to pull herself upright. She shook her head, instantly regretting the reflex. She braced herself against the headboard for support, and the rolling of the room leveled off. In measured steps she made her way to the vanity sink. Elle checked her reflection and shrugged. Her strawberry-auburn halo of curls had turned into an off-red bird's nest while she slept. Her green eyes felt dry and puffy, as did her mouth.

Ellie, girl, we are not as young as we used to be, she thought, noticing the scratchy feel and bitter aftertaste on her tongue.

"And, come on, we don't even like whiskey," she added aloud.

She crossed the room to the small bank of open windows overlooking the lawn between the two cottages and the main house. The sill was wet from the night's intense downpour. Despite her hazy recollection of the previous evening, Elle did remember thunder—lots of it. Closing the windows helped to stifle Lyle's early morning efforts on the bagpipes.

Elle imagined this tune might be "Loch Lomond." Or maybe not.

Over the lawn and a border of dark green alder trees, Aldermire rose silhouetted against the morning sky. No lights yet appeared in the upper-story windows, suggesting the family was still sleeping off the previous night's excitement. For nearly 250 years, the great house had held court on Roan Island, a brick and mortar reminder of the once prosperous Clan MacUspaig.

Elle traced the house's many chimneys and gables with her eye. For rock bottom, she thought it was a pretty good way to start a day.

"You just have to make better choices, and keep moving forward," she said softly but with conviction. "Last night was a good choice. Not an easy choice, but a good choice. Gotta start somewhere."

She sat on the side of the bed and pieced together what she could of the previous evening. As her memory cleared, she fought the powerful urge to cocoon herself under a forgiving pile of blankets. The struggle ended as the cottage's landline rang.

Elle again looked at the nightstand clock in disbelief, then picked up the receiver.

"Hello?" she said. She hoped there was enough displeasure in her voice for whomever had the gall to call before breakfast on a Saturday.

Her mother's voice greeted her. "Ellie, it's Mama. Did I wake you up?" For the second time in as many days, Elle thought she might have better luck with Lyle's bagpipes.

"Mama, it's early," she said. As the words passed her lips, she knew it was fruitless. Gavina Walker Cunningham accepted no pleas for mercy and took no prisoners.

"I haven't spoken to you in three days," her mother continued. "With all the storms and you out there in the middle of the river, I have been beside myself. You have no idea how much I worry about you."

"There's nothing to worry about," Elle said. "What could happen out here on Roan? I'm safely tucked away in one of the cottages, and my job is keeping me busy." It was a small word, but once it slipped past her lips, she wished she could take it back. Elle detected a brief pause before her mother responded.

She knew her mother was searching for the right words. Elle braced herself.

"Do you *really* consider that a job?" Gavina asked.

"Wow," Elle said too quickly. "We are just going to jump right into this?"

"Isn't this more of a hobby that got a little out of control?" Her mama continued without pause. "Elle, honey, you need to find a real job. You're nearly forty, single, no children and now, no real job. Just because the university cut you loose doesn't mean you can't find something better. Every night I stay up worrying about you."

This was not a conversation she could win, and Elle knew it.

"I love my job. I love my life," she said.

"But how can you live off what you earn?" Gavina asked. "You really need to start thinking about the future."

"Mama, I earn plenty. I have my research. I have my writing," Elle said. She scoured her mind for more weight to add to the list. "I have my freedom. I have the admiration of my peers."

"Elle, really," her mother said with a carefully cultivated blend of concern and impatience. "When was the last time you could pay for dinner with cash, credit card or professional respect? If you could, you'd be out of debt in no time."

Elle thought about a response that would, she was sure, have sounded more biting than intended. A scuffle on the other end of the call stopped her short.

"Hey, baby girl," came her sister's cheerful twang through the receiver. "Sorry about that. I'm at Mama's to take her grocery shopping. I turned around for half a second, and she was on the phone like brown sugar on oatmeal. I've never seen her move that fast."

"Why does she only call me when you're around?" Elle asked, fully relieved to hear Alana's voice.

"Maybe if she talks loud enough, it's like she's lecturing us both with one breath," Lana guessed. "Think of all the time it saves her."

Elle laughed. "Efficiency is her thing," she said. "Okay, so what's up with Mama and the crack of dawn phone call?"

"Were you out of bed?"

"Barely," Elle admitted.

"Thinking about going back to bed?"

"Most definitely."

"Okay," Lana offered. "I'll give you the short version. Lainie Daleroch was at the movies last night in Wilmington. She talked to Anna Haymaker, something about some mysterious dinner party that was happening at Aldermire. Anna told her sister, Frances, who works for Mama under Terri Otto's crew. She texted Terri, and Terri texted Mama. Mama got curious."

Elle's head was starting to spin again. "That was the short version?" Elle asked. She thought for a second. "But Mama never asked me about the dinner."

"She got sidetracked," Lana suggested. "Or she never wanted to know about the dinner. She just needed an excuse to call you. It provides a nice pretense to recap the list of disappointments she's always keeping."

"Well, this time she just started with the list," Elle conceded. "Like you said, think of all the time it saves her."

"So, since we're on the subject, what was up with this dinner?" Lana asked.

Elle managed to grimace and laugh out loud at once. "It was mostly the family here on Roan and a few of the local higher-ups from Saint Andrews and Wilmington."

"Anyone I know?"

"Not sure about that, but they seemed to know Mama," Elle replied. "One of them introduced me as one of Vee's daughters. You could see the wheels turning. 'Which one is she? The jailbird or the lesbian?'"

Lana laughed. "I hope you kept them guessing."

"Nah, I just dazzled them with my research until the evening turned south. Honestly, Lana, it was a bloodbath. I'm going to write an entire book about it," Elle said, only half joking.

"Bloodbath? Ellie, you can't tease me with something like that. I need details. Lots and lots and lots of details."

"I thought you guys were going shopping," Elle said.

"Mama's walking out to the car. She can wait; five more minutes won't kill her. She'll figure out how to roll down the windows."

"Okay, real quick. Stuart is divorcing his wife, Megan," Elle said. "She used to be Megan Bloom. She was in my year at school, maybe too young for you to have known. Anyway, he's kicking the whole family out, selling the island and the house, and he's shutting the whole thing down. Dropped them all like bombshells at dinner. It was pandemonium."

"And this is the same Stuart that you, um, knew from before?" Lana asked with a hint of mischief in her voice.

"You know the answer to that one," Elle replied. "Anyway, once he told everyone that..." Elle's voice trailed off. "Oh, crap."

"Ellie, what's the matter?" Lana asked.

Sitting on the bed, Elle noticed a long brown leather strap resting on the reading chair next to the cottage door. An oblong tasseled pouch made of matching leather was tucked underneath. Her heart fell as she recognized Stuart's sporran, a forgotten memento from the previous evening. Elle tried wishing it away with no success.

"Lana, it's nothing serious," Elle said with haste. "I've got to run to the main house for a minute. Forgot something."

"Okay, I need to check on Mama anyway," her sister said. "Give me a call later. I can never get you by cell out there so call me when you get a chance. Love you, Ellie."

"Love you, too." She hung up the phone and was dressed in sweats in less than thirty seconds.

With Stuart's sporran tucked under one arm, Elle stepped out of the red cottage and into the chill morning air. The late-night thunderstorm was just what the island needed, she thought, a good downpour to wash away the tensions of the previous evening.

Elle snapped the screen door shut and took a quick step toward Aldermire. She resolved to be in and out of the main house before anyone noticed. The thought of a warm meal slowed her step, and she revised her plan. *First drop the sporran, then grab some breakfast,* she thought. Whatever Lainie was cooking up would be far more satisfying than the dry cereal she had squirreled away at the cottage.

Elle took two more steps and paused. Something wasn't right. Despite her haste, she turned to retrace her steps. There was something amiss with the white cottage. She couldn't put her finger on the specific change, but something *had* changed. On cue, a morning breeze swung the cottage screen door open. The gentle movement caught her eye like a warning light.

"Odd, that screen door was closed last night," she said to herself. "I latched it myself." Despite her concern, she knew she had a bigger problem to deal with. The white cottage mystery would wait.

In the sixty seconds it took Elle to reach the west terrace, the screen door was a distant memory. The morning air was crisp and clear. A gentle, brackish sea breeze drifted through the barrier islands and across the Cape Fear River. As the leaves of the alders bobbed in rhythm, a jittery weathervane atop the main house tried to make sense of the approaching storm winds.

Roan Island was just shy of three miles south of Eagle Island and the village of Saint Andrews. Roan was even closer to the city of Wilmington's west shore, but to Elle the island felt like a safe haven in a distant ocean. The few visits she had paid Aldermire as a child were hectic times, always during a school trip or a special dinner.

Like many of their Wilmington contemporaries, Elle and Alana would slip on black suede ghillies and compete in amateur Highland dancing trials and occasionally perform at Scottish events in the Cape Fear region. During more than one Burns Night celebration, the pair had danced at Aldermire to the delight of the assembled guests. Accompanied by a master piper, the girls would complete intricate step dance routines that required endless patience, skill and stamina.

To Gavina Walker Cunningham's chagrin, her daughters had no particular talent or passion for the art. While both girls had the requisite stamina, neither had the patience or the skill. At first chance, Alana would slip away to wander the gardens. Her younger sister would sequester herself in the estate's library, reveling in stories of Scottish clans from the new world and the old.

Today, Elle thought, was a world apart from those previous visits. This was something magical—a place where nothing could touch her. It was her first opportunity to enjoy the estate and its environs in peace; it was a welcomed change. She could understand why the last few MacUspaigs stayed hunkered down here.

As she climbed the wide steps to the terrace, the hallowed silence was spoiled by a muffled howl. She reached the patio and abandoned any pretense of stealth. She gave a resigned wave to the on-again, off-again guard dog posted just behind the library's bay window. *Six weeks in and Angus still doesn't recognize me,* she thought with a shrug.

Distracted by the hound, Elle took a moment to collect her thoughts and assess the confusing scene not thirty feet in front of her. A body lay passed out, face down, on the grand terrace approaching the library's French doors. Stuart MacUspaig—and she was certain it was Stuart—was still dressed in his full kilt and jacket, and his clothing was visibly wet from the storm hours before.

Like the white cottage screen door just moments before, there was something not quite right about the sight. Her logical subconscious attempted to sequence the elements into some pattern or order. Stuart was unconscious, yet the rain had not roused him. His waistcoat and kilt were a matching kit, yet the jacket was a far darker version of the traditional MacUspaig tartan. He had been fine just six hours ago, yet now there was a dagger hilt jutting from the center of his back.

"Oh my God," Elle said out loud as the horror of what she was seeing progressed from conjecture to reality. "Stuart?"

For a suspended moment, Elle regarded the grand terrace as an absurd tableau, a hyper-realistic painting by an Italian master whose name she should know. In its own defense, her brain shifted into a higher gear, capturing every detail to be replayed over and over again during the coming nights.

She immediately noted that Stuart was dressed as he had been when he left her cottage the night before. He had fallen forward, not unusual for a man who's had too much whiskey. In fact, his body seemed relaxed, she imagined, almost lackadaisical. There were no other wounds visible across his back, suggesting the dagger had entered only once. No hesitance or practice strokes were evident.

The dagger was familiar to Elle. It was long and plainly adorned. The portion of the blade not embedded in Stuart's back was some kind of hard metal—steel, she guessed. The short, carved handle was jet black, perhaps bog oak. The familiarity nagged at her memory. She had seen it before, but she was unable to place exactly where.

Her final rational observation was Stuart's wet clothing. He had left her cottage before the rainstorm, she recalled. The blood on the ground formed an intricate lacework pattern as it snaked along the crevice between the patio pavers. A larger bloodstain next to the body—next to Stuart—had darker edges, although the center had largely been washed away. Whatever befell him must have happened before or during the night's storm.

At that moment, Elle's focus splintered as a woman's screams brought her back into the moment.

From the patio door directly to the kitchen, Lainie Daleroch's keening shook the sleepy estate to life. Several faces appeared at windows as additional alarms were raised. Elle heard door latches in the distance, and family members emerged on the second-floor balcony overlooking the grand terrace.

In the center of the confusion, she felt both helpless and desperate to move. The eyes once again upon her implored her to take action. She stood over Stuart's motionless form as the seconds passed without another sound from within Aldermire.

The French doors to her left burst open with a crack, and Lyle MacUspaig sprinted to her side. As he approached his older brother's body, he joined Elle in inaction. They looked at one another in shock and, uncertain what to do next, knelt in unison. Elle reached out and felt Stuart's neck.

"No pulse," she said so only Lyle could hear.

With shock blossoming across his face, he reached instinctively for the dirk protruding from his brother's body. Elle's hand smacked his away, his surprise giving way to understanding as he drew back.

"Oh, God," he said. "I am so sorry. I don't know why I did that." He paused, dumbfounded. "It just looks so...wrong. It shouldn't be there."

"This *is* wrong," Elle replied. "I don't know what the hell happened, but I need you to keep it together. Go make sure the family is as okay as they can be. Are we good?" she asked, placing her hand firmly on his shoulder. She didn't wait for a response.

"Have Leith call the police immediately," she said. "I'll stay with the...with Stuart. And for the love of God, keep everyone together and in the house."

As she had for the past six weeks, Elle felt like an outsider. The voices echoing from within the great house were a growing cacophony of grief and disbelief. The family members were experiencing shock in its many forms, but they were still experiencing it as a family. Elle knew she was better served standing guard outside.

She watched Lyle's progress through the open doors and into the library where the other inhabitants of Aldermire had gathered. A slight movement to her right caught Elle's notice, and she turned to see a shocked Megan MacUspaig watching her from the library's bay window. The new widow's eyes slowly drifted from her dead husband to Elle's face, then to the sporran still tucked beneath Elle's right arm. Elle could see the grief and shock churn into a barely contained rage.

"Damn," she muttered.

Leith Daleroch's voice came from the open French doors. "Elle, my dear, can you please come inside?"

She maintained her watch a moment longer, and he repeated his request. "I've called the police, and they are on their way from Saint Andrews. Should be only fifteen minutes or so by boat," he said. "We don't know what happened to Stuart, but until we do, I'd feel better if you were here with us. Please, my dear." He reached out a hand to emphasize his point.

Elle was reluctant to face the family, but hovering over Stuart didn't provide a reasonable alternative. She acquiesced, looked over his body one last time, and crossed the patio through the library and into the dining room.

The group regarded her arrival with a mixture of disinterest and disdain. Hendry MacUspaig sat at the head of the large table, as unmoving as he was during dinner the evening before. It was clear that Megan's efforts had ended with the meal; half-filled plates and empty chafing dishes still cluttered the tables. To Elle, that dinner felt a lifetime away.

Leith returned to sit beside his daughter, holding Lainie's hand as she cried into a cloth napkin. The girl reflexively tucked strands of long blond hair behind her ears after each sob, her blue eyes now red with grief. *In looks, if not strength, she certainly is her father's daughter,* Elle thought.

Angus sprawled at her feet, oblivious to the turmoil around him. He slept on his back, his stubby legs pointing at the open beam ceiling and his ears splayed out to an impressive length. His soft snoring occasionally skipped a beat as he yipped at some dreamt intruder.

At the far end of the room, Megan MacUspaig looked away as Elle entered. Her only son, Cade, had returned from the previous night's trip to the mainland. He, too, ignored Elle, not from contempt but instead from a concern for his mother's wellbeing.

Only eighteen, Cade was already broad-shouldered, like his mother. Also like Megan, Cade had short dark hair and expressive eyes. If his eyes held any sympathy for his recently deceased stepfather, Elle thought, they certainly didn't show it.

The final pair, Lyle and Caroline MacUspaig, colluded in the opposite corner. Their shock was evident despite the hushed tones of their conversation. Elle thought Lyle clearly looked upset, although Caroline's wheels were already turning.

Of the different couples now sequestered throughout the room, Elle noticed that no one seemed interested in what was happening outside of his or her own pairing. Stuart's death was already dividing the house along lines of family and personal loyalty. Once again, Elle felt like the odd woman out.

Unsure where to move, she chose a central chair at the dining table. She felt it was a safe and respectable distance from the various camps now staking their territory around the room. As was his custom, it fell to the Daleroch patriarch to break the silence.

"Elle, my dear, could you tell us what happened to poor Stuart?" he asked with a patient graciousness.

She shrugged. "I think you all know what I do," she said. "I walked over to the house for breakfast and found Stuart a few minutes ago. He was stabbed, that much was plain. I think I've seen the knife before, but I can't remember where." Elle ran her fingers through her hair, searching for any other information she could provide. She came up empty-handed. "I'm sorry, but this is just so far beyond belief."

"Well, we will let the police take over from here," Leith said. At the mention of the police, Lyle and Caroline broke from their huddle.

"That's just one nightmare that needs to be fixed," Lyle said to the room. "Daleroch, you're our attorney. What happens to the house now? The island? I don't mean to be indelicate, but had Stuart already sold the place or was that just a standing threat?"

"He simply couldn't have done that to us," Caroline added in a naked bid for sympathy. "This is our home. Oh, and everyone else's as well, of course. Well, everyone else except Elle."

She gave Elle a wan smile. "I don't mean to single you out, but it's true." She closed with a shrug of helplessness to minimize the impact of her words.

"Caroline, this may not be the right time," Leith said. "There are too many unanswered questions."

"Is the handle black?"

The voice caught the family off guard. It was hoarse and feeble. Elle turned her head to the end of the table and was shocked to see Hendry MacUspaig staring her down. He expected an answer.

"Young woman, I asked you a very simple question," he said. "Is the handle black?"

"Yes, it is," Elle replied. "Maybe bog oak or some other hardwood."

"Aye, I know it," Hendry said. His tone suggested he found pleasure in the full attention of the couples around the room.

His dark brown eyes flashed black under the dining room's elaborate chandelier. The old man seemed to be savoring the moment, waiting a few seconds longer than necessary to continue.

"You all would know it if you paid a damn bit of attention to our family's history," the patriarch spat. "Lyle, how many times have you stood in front of the fireplace in my study? A dozen times? A hundred?"

A brief note of recognition lit his son's face. "The two on the mantle?" Lyle asked. "The dagger and the club?"

"It's a dirk and a mace, you damned fool. Not that you'd know the difference," Hendry countered. "Those two have been in the family for 300 years, maybe more. Now, no longer."

"Hendry, what do you mean by 'no longer'?" Leith asked.

"Aye, they are missing from where they've sat for all these years," the old man replied with a note of satisfaction in his voice. "Aye, both. Not that it matters now."

The room descended into an awkward silence. The family members regarded each other slowly and with suspicion. As the reality of Stuart's death lay before them, no one dared speak first.

"Okay, fine, I'll say it," Elle said at last. "If that's the dagger from Hendry's study, and I think we can agree that it is, we know one thing about what happened last night. Whoever did this to Stuart was obviously in the house before going out to the terrace."

Hendry replied, "Of course, that much was obvious." Elle ignored the dig; the man's son was dead.

"If the alarm was set and Angus was downstairs, I believe we can take this a step further," she continued.

"It is a logical, if uncomfortable, conclusion," Leith said.

Lainie Daleroch looked up from the table with a confused expression. "What did we conclude? Did I miss something?" she asked.

With a sigh, Elle concluded, "Stuart's killer is likely sitting in this room."

"And that is an excellent reason for us to now defer to the local constabulary," Leith added with subtle urgency. "This is a matter for their expertise and not, I'm sorry, my dear, for our suppositions—no matter how well meaning."

As Leith finished, a chorus of unfamiliar voices arose outside on the grand terrace, and the family moved en masse to the library. A group of men and women in matching windbreakers were circling Stuart's body and cordoning off the immediate area. Angus stirred from his slumber long enough to bark a delayed warning. The police had arrived.

4

A dog barks when his master is attacked. I would be a coward if I saw that God's truth is attacked and yet would remain silent.

— John Calvin

A tall, dark-haired man with a youthful face surveyed the patio from the top step leading into the house. He snapped orders to his colleagues and turned to enter the library. While his fellow officers marked the scene with orange cones and yellow tape, he tapped his shoes with care against the door jam and made his way through the library into the warmth of the dining room. When his eyes fell on Elle, he stopped short. He glanced once more around the room and introduced himself.

"Good morning, all," he said with a deep baritone that didn't quite fit his youthful features. "I am Detective Jonah Tanner with the New Hanover County Sheriff's Department. I know this has been a huge shock for you all, but please help us by letting us do our job. If you all can stay put here, we'll be done outside as soon as the coroner arrives. I'll need to speak to each of you the moment we are through, so please, again, just stay put for the time being."

Leith and Caroline nodded in agreement. The rest sat, unmoving and without emotion.

"One question," he added. "I need to know who found Mr. MacUspaig."

The group turned in unison to look at Elle, and she responded by raising her hand slowly. Detective Tanner took a deep breath and shook his head.

"Right," he said with care. "Elle, I need to speak to you outside for just a moment. Everyone else, remember, stay put." His words had an immediate impact on the energy of the room. Eyebrows raised and looks were exchanged in silence.

Elle tried to ignore the questions that would be asked in her absence. Yes, she was on a first-name basis with the young officer. Yes, there must a perfectly good reason. Jonah motioned her outside, and she followed his lead without making eye contact with the others.

He led her across the patio, past the section cordoned off for Stuart's body. When he was sure their conversation would be out of earshot, Jonah turned to face Elle. On his youthful features, the anger read more as annoyance.

"What the hell, Mackay?" he said. "You found MacUspaig's body? I don't know where to start."

"Let me start it for you," she said, her hackles rising. "I don't care what you think you know, but I'll tell you exactly what I can. Just stop rolling your eyes. Deal?"

He shook his head. "No deals, you know that. Just make it fast and keep it honest."

"Now wait, Jonah. When have I ever lied to you?" she asked. "I may have been a huge pain in your ass, but I have *always* owned up to anything I've ever done." She held his gaze while neither spoke.

He ran his fingers through his short brown hair. "Sorry," he said. "That was out of bounds. Honestly, we don't get a whole lot of homicides out on the islands. This is the first since my promotion, and I can't afford to screw this up. So when I walked in and saw you sitting there... I don't know, it just hit me wrong."

"I have that effect on a lot of people around here."

"Well, let's see," Jonah replied. "In the past two years you've had one disturbing the peace, two public intoxications, a forced eviction, a bar fight and at least three other calls that didn't result in charges or citations."

"Not that you're counting," Elle said.

"Yeah, not that I'm counting. You're just lucky your mother has some kind of spell over the sheriff. I know she and Hopkirk go back twenty or thirty years, but there's going to be a limit to what he can overlook."

Elle shrugged. "Trust me. I know I'm running out of second chances."

Jonah nodded. "I just hadn't seen you in, what, six months? I hoped you were getting things straightened out."

"Actually, I'm getting there," Elle said. "That was a real rough patch for me. No excuses, but I think that my life has turned a corner. As far as I know, whatever happened to Stuart had nothing to do with me."

"I'm truly glad to hear that," he said with a smile. "So, want to tell me what I missed?"

"I'll give you the short version," she replied. "The details can wait until you're ready for them. Last night at dinner, Stuart dropped a bomb. He's divorcing his wife and selling the estate. From what I could tell, no one else was aware this was going down with the possible exception of his lawyer."

"I'll need the lawyer's phone number."

"I'll make it easy for you," she replied. "Leith Daleroch is the older fellow sitting next to the blond girl. He's the one who called the police. Start with him."

Jonah took a few notes in a small notebook. "How'd the family take it?"

Elle shrugged. "Talk to them, and you'll find out quick enough," she replied. "They aren't a shy group."

"Mrs. MacUspaig. She's the tall brunette, right?" he asked.

"Oh yeah, that's Megan."

"Any idea if she was looking to skip judge and jury then go straight to executioner?" he asked. "I saw the looks she was giving you; I don't think she's a fan. Anything else I should know?"

"I'm getting to it," she said. "Several years ago, and this was well before they were married, Stuart and I had, well, let's call it a *thing*. Nothing serious, just an acquaintances-with-benefits arrangement. Since he told her, I don't think she's ever trusted me around him."

"And that's it?" he asked, leaning into her as though his height gave his request more urgency.

"Give me a second," Elle replied. "There's no easy way to say this, but after dinner last night, Stuart stopped by my cottage. I'm staying on the island in one of the guest houses. I think he was looking to rekindle the past."

He whistled. "Elle, that's not good."

"Don't get ahead of me," she said. "Nothing happened. And I mean *nothing* happened. He left maybe ten minutes later a very disappointed man. I own my mistakes, and I try not to repeat them."

"Mrs. MacUspaig knows about all this?"

"She might know," Elle said, then reconsidered. "Or at least she thinks she knows what happened."

Jonah cocked one eyebrow. "Now, that's not good for her."

"The thing is I don't think she had any inkling about last night until this morning," Elle said. "I can't give you anything more specific than that. It's just a feeling. I've known Megan since we were kids, and she doesn't hide her emotions well. If she had known what he was up to last night, I'd be the one lying on the terrace right now. She would have taken pictures, sent out invites, probably set the entire thing to music and fireworks."

"I'll take that under advisement," Jonah replied.

"One more thing," Elle added. "Stuart could be a horse's ass, but he was a decent guy. He's one of the few people from my past who gave me a second chance when a lot of doors in my life had already closed. I'm back at work and have a roof over my head because of Stuart MacUspaig's generosity. I wasn't crazy about him, but I owe him more than I can say."

"Understood."

"And, Jonah, I want to give you fair warning," she said. "You need to find out who did this, because I'm gonna be looking on my own."

"Elle, you know this is my job as much as I know telling you to stand down will do precious little good," he replied. "Do what you have to do, just please stay out of our way. Once you get past all the trouble and mischief, I think you're a smart person and you're a good person. Please don't make me jam you up because you stepped on the wrong toes. Are we square?"

"We're square."

As she acclimated to the unnatural quiet of the library, Elle felt like an errant child returning from the principal's office. Angus had watched her enter, his ears perking up in anticipation.

After a leisurely stretch, the hound sauntered over and fell at her feet. Though they had been whispering upon her arrival, Lyle and Caroline regarded each other without speaking. The rest of the family sat in weary silence.

At last, Hendry MacUspaig spoke. "I have no interest in dying here, surrounded by you fools," he said in gravid tones. "Lainie, please help me to my room. Leith, if the police inquire, you'll earn your keep and inform them where I've gone. If they don't like it, be certain to tell them that I don't give a damn."

"Hendry, I'm sure it will be fine," Leith replied. "Let's all agree to stay in the house or, in your case Elle, dear, your cottage. I'm certain the young detective meant we shouldn't leave the island."

As Lainie helped the MacUspaig patriarch up from his chair and out of the room, Cade made no excuses and departed for his room. Megan soon followed without a word. Alone with their thoughts, Lyle, Caroline, Leith and Elle struggled to make conversation. After a few minutes of watching the police comb the grand terrace or look for a decent cell phone signal, Lyle broke the silence.

"As much as I hate to say it, I think Elle is right," he said.

"About?" Leith asked.

"About Stuart's killer being one of us," he said. "Right after dinner, Dr. Buchanan-Berman and the others left on the ferry. It was waiting for us at the dock when I walked down to see them off. Cade and Lainie had our boat up at Saint Andrews, and there aren't many other ways to get onto Roan."

"But someone else could have been here on the island. Couldn't they?" Caroline asked. Elle knew the young woman was fishing for alternatives. Another plausible explanation might help her avoid the unpleasant thought of a murderer in their midst.

"I suppose so, but it isn't likely," her husband said. "To Elle's point, the alarm is always set and Angus barks at anyone he doesn't know. Hell, he barks at most of the people he does know. He'd have raised all kinds of Cain if a stranger had approached Stuart on the terrace. Lainie swears the dog was still sleeping under this table when she and Cade got home last night."

"That suggests that whoever killed Stuart was already in the house and well known to Angus," Elle concluded. At the mention of the hound dog, she reached down and scratched his waiting jowls. He returned the favor with a slobber-drenched lick with his tongue.

"There's something else," Elle said. "I mentioned the dagger because I think it's important."

"How so?" Leith asked.

Elle looked to the kitchen, then back to the others. "If you were a stranger set on killing someone, where would you go for a knife? Think about it. I certainly wouldn't break in, head to the top floor, enter a locked study, steal a family heirloom that I didn't know existed, slip back downstairs and corner my victim on a huge outdoor terrace. It just doesn't make sense."

Leith nodded. "Excellent point, my dear. The kitchen is home to any number of suitable knives, and Hendry's collection of arms in the front foyer provides an endless variety of deadly implements. The dagger may have been chosen with as much care as was poor Stuart."

As he finished, motion on the patio caught Elle's eye. The coroner and her assistant lifted Stuart's covered body onto a wheeled gurney. In silence the four mourners watched as the officers rolled the former lord of the household down the river rock path to the waiting pontoon boat. This time it was Caroline who interrupted their repose.

"I just can't believe he's gone," she said. After what Elle considered too short a wait, Caroline added, "I don't mean to sound crass, but is anyone else hungry?"

Isolated in the comfort and quiet of her cottage, Elle felt a deep need to connect with someone who knew her. On the third ring, Lana answered her phone.

"Baby girl, what is going on down there?" Lana asked before Elle could even say hello.

"Did Mama tell you?" Elle asked. She knew the answer.

"She has been calling me every five minutes, swears she is too upset to call you directly," her sister said. "Sheriff Hopkirk rang her up the instant he heard you were staying at Aldermire. She's on her way over here now. So, spill it, what happened?"

Elle chose her words with care. "Lana, remember last night when I said dinner was a bloodbath? Turns out it was a very poor choice of words."

"Clever wordplay aside, just tell me you're okay," Lana said.

"I'm fine," she replied. "Stuart, not so much. Someone stabbed him last night on the big patio behind Aldermire. He didn't make it. I found him this morning."

"Oh my God, Elle. Are you sure you're alright?"

"I'm a little shaken up, but I'm better than could probably be expected," she said. "I'd just like to know why. And who. Lana, I have no idea who did it, but my gut says it was someone in the family. We are all staying put until the police can talk to us one by one."

"Ellie, you're leaving something out," she said. Elle wasn't sure if her sister was as certain as she sounded, but Elle knew she owed Lana her honesty.

"Likely minutes before he died, Stuart stopped by my cottage," Elle replied. "He was feeling, let's say, amorous."

"Ellie, please tell me you didn't."

"Hey, I'm all for an innocent roll in the hay, but I'm not stupid," Elle said, trying to sound offended. "He was sent packing with his tail between his legs."

"Well, it wasn't his tail I was worried about," Lana replied. Her sister was making light of a dead man's final minutes, but Elle knew it was an honest attempt to elevate her mood. "That's just horrible about Stuart. Still, I'm proud of you, baby girl."

Despite the unimaginable start to her day, Elle found her sister's good humor infectious. For nearly forty years, Lana had been an endless source of care, comradery and stability. This morning, Elle felt she needed that lifeline more than ever.

"What was so worthy of your admiration?" she asked, returning Lana's good-natured tone with her own.

"Little sister, you said 'no.' That's a big step forward," Lana replied with an audible smirk. "I can't believe I even have to check, but please tell me you're not giving up on men."

"Is that so far beyond belief?" Elle asked. "You assume that I need a man in my life to find true happiness. How little you know me." She clucked her tongue in mock disapproval. "If you can give up men, why can't I?"

Lana laughed.

"You never know," Elle continued. "Maybe I would make a fantastic lesbian. You make it look so easy."

Lana laughed again, louder this time, as words seemed to fail her. That laugh, Elle felt in her heart, was one of her favorite sounds.

"Ellie, I'm not sure you understand how this works. I can't give up something I never started to begin with. Let's just agree you'd be setting yourself up for disappointment."

"Don't you believe in me?" Elle teased.

"Oh, I believe you and I believe *in* you. But there's a flaw in your plan, and I can sum it up with one word," Lana replied. "Men. Ellie, dear, even when you're saying 'no,' you are far, far too enamored with the male of the species."

"Damn it, Lana," Elle replied. "I hate it when you're right. I'd make a lackluster lesbian."

Lana chuckled. "Stick with what you know, little sister."

They shared a final laugh, then a moment of silence. "Thanks for taking my mind off of all of this," Elle said. "I don't know that it's all hit home just yet. Stuart's body just lying there—it doesn't seem real."

"Any time, baby girl," Lana replied. "Just promise me you're going to be alright."

Before Elle could answer, she heard a familiar commotion in the background. As her sister's voice receded from the telephone handset, Elle heard her call, "I held her off as long as I could, Ellie."

"Really, Ellie." Mama's voice cut through her like a brisk wind. "Canoodling with a married man. Again. The first time wasn't enough of a disaster? And don't deny it. I just got off the phone with the sheriff."

Elle knew her best defense was to stick to the facts. "Mama," she said with what little calm she could manage, "Stuart is dead, and his final night was filled with rejection. Nothing happened. No canoodling. Nada. Zero. Nothing."

The phone went silent for several long seconds. "Ellie, I just worry about you more than you'll ever know," she said. "You don't always make the best life choices. That weekend with the Connors fellow didn't turn out as you planned, did it?"

"Mama, this is not the time." Clearly, to Gavina, this was the time.

"Let's be honest. You already had the scarlet 'A,'" her mother said. "Ellie, did you really need to work harder for an A+?"

"Mama, you're not helping."

"Elle, dear, your life is starting over again, and I want you to step off on the right foot. All I am saying is that you picked one hell of a time to become an overachiever."

After a second scuffle on the other end of the phone, Lana's voice returned. "Never once in her life has she fit 'All I am saying' into one breath. You know this is just her first teachable moment in what promises to be a week-long homily on the sanctity of marital fidelity."

Elle replied without levity, "Easy words from a woman who was widowed three years in. She never had time to screw up her marriage."

"That's not fair, Ellie."

"And those are easy words from the perfect daughter," Elle replied. She immediately regretted her response. "Sorry, Lana. You just have no idea what it feels like to be square in her crosshairs."

Despite the barb, Lana was willing to let her sister's comments slide. "In my defense, I've had my share of scrutiny from Mama. You just made my screw-ups seem amateur by comparison. At my best, I couldn't outshine you when you got on a roll." Elle knew where this conversation was going. It was one they had had several times before.

"The first and only night I ever broke curfew, you wrapped one of her maid-mobiles around our oak tree," Lana said.

"Between you, me and that car, I'm the only one who got off without a scratch."

"Mama has so exaggerated that night," Elle replied. "It's hard to wrap a car around a tree at five miles per hour. She's taken plenty of literary license with that one. After five or six tellings, it went from a bent fender to a high-speed police chase across our front lawn."

Lana laughed and said, "True, but how the hell did you know how to drive a car at thirteen years old?"

"If I had known how to drive, you think I would have hit that tree?"

Lana chuckled again. "Excellent point."

"The arcade games just made it look so easy," Elle replied. "And maybe I was venting some youthful aggression."

"Well, the whole 'angry, rebellious teen' thing suited you well," the older sister said. "And you really sank your teeth into the role."

"I hate to admit it, but maybe Mama is right," Elle said. "Maybe I am an overachiever after all."

Lana laughed a final time. "I'll say it again, little sister, stick with what you know." She paused. "Love you, Ellie. Stay safe for me."

5

The world is full of obvious things which nobody by any chance ever observes.

— Arthur Conan Doyle,
The Hound of the Baskervilles

Resting on the cottage's lone bed, Elle drifted in and out of sleep. In her mind's slumbering eye she relived the discovery of Stuart's body. As her subconscious paced a slow circle around his lifeless form, the dagger's handle protruded like the gnomon of a grotesque sundial.

In her dream, the morning sun arced through the sky, and the handle cast its shadow across his still back. That steady progression, however, was soon joined by another, more subtle movement. The deep reds and greens of the MacUspaig tartan began to curl and writhe. They mixed freely with the grass between the paver stones and the rivulets of blood that flowed from the open wound.

The organic hues and threads overlapped one another with a hypnotic rhythm forming an intricate tapestry, a pictorial history of Stuart, Lyle, Hendry, Eachann, Beitiris and the countless other MacUspaig family members who predeceased them. Elle watched with fascination as dozens of tiny pixelated lives played out before her. It was life, she thought, and death and art and beauty.

As the tapestry wove itself toward the dagger, it began to fray. The gash in Stuart's back became a hole in the fabric, in the family itself. In what may have been generations, hours, or simply seconds, this pictorial history of Clan MacUspaig unwound before Elle's eyes.

A closer look revealed to Elle that the threads were already bare and weak. While Stuart's death was certainly the immediate cause of the unweaving, her soul told her that it wasn't the beginning. *This weakness, this tattering,* she thought, *started somewhere in the past.*

As she continued to examine the tapestry in reverse, she found herself in a race against time. She scoured the fragile threads for some clue, and as she searched the scenes fell to scraps in her hands.

If I can just search faster, she thought in her dream. The answer only moments from her grasp, she was jolted awake by the ring of the cottage's landline.

"Mackay?" Jonah's voice asked. Without waiting for her response, he continued, "We are finishing up with the lawyer, and I need you here at the big house."

Elle stretched. She thought of a stinging retort, then thought again. "Give me five minutes."

"Make it fast," he said. "I have to talk to each of you, and there's food if you're hungry. I don't think anyone's eaten since this morning."

"Food? I'll be there in four."

Four minutes later, Elle stood in the kitchen at Aldermire surrounded by the remaining MacUspaigs. Jonah was true to his word—Lainie had managed a healthy selection of cold sandwiches and doctored leftovers from the night before. Leith was still speaking with the young detective and his colleagues in the dining room. The rest of the family sat around the island counter, waiting for a turn with the investigators.

As Elle ate, Caroline talked out loud. Her nervous energy, Elle observed, usually found an outlet in endless chatter. Her words continued, although the others scarcely noticed.

"So does this mean we still have to leave Roan?" Caroline asked to no one in particular. "Lyle and I can't live this way, not knowing whether or not Aldermire still belongs to the family." After several seconds of silence, she got a reaction. Lyle shook his head and moved from the counter to the kitchen window.

"This is total insanity," she said, changing tactics. "I simply won't be able to sleep until I know who did this to poor Stuart."

The mention of Stuart's name snapped the group back from their divergent trains of thought. They regarded one another in silence as Cade stood to retrieve a pad of paper from the small desk beneath the kitchen phone.

"Look, we know how this works," Cade began. "Miss Mackay is probably right. It was one of you who did this."

"Well, to be fair, it could have been you, too," Caroline replied. She added a smile as though to turn the accusation into a careless observation.

"Back the hell off," Megan snapped. She stood and pushed her chair back to emphasize the point. "Caroline, don't even start. Lainie and Cade didn't come back until the rain ended. They were still on Eagle Island long after Stuart was probably killed."

"Megan, I was just trying to consider all options. Cade, I hope you know I meant no offense at all."

"Aunt Caroline, it's fine," he replied. He tapped the pen against the pad of paper. "And that's what I want to hear from you all. I know where I was last night, and we can rule out the dog. So where were each of you?"

"Aye, you're a bright lad." Hendry spoke without looking at the family gathered around him. "If I didn't already know better, I'd swear you were born a MacUspaig, not just borrowing the good name."

Elle nodded. "I agree, it's not a bad idea. Might as well get our stories straight since the police will be asking us the same questions in just a few minutes."

Caroline and Lyle exchanged a quick glance. Megan shrugged.

"So, how about it?" Elle said. "I think we can agree that Cade and Lainie were in Saint Andrews. I'll go next. I was in the red cottage."

"Were you alone?" Megan asked with an unblinking stare. "Can anyone vouch for you?"

"The only one who could is now dead," Elle replied and turned to the group. "Just so you all know, Stuart stopped by the cottage maybe fifteen minutes after I left Aldermire. He only stayed for five or ten minutes, then left. He said he was going back to the house." She rubbed her temples and considered the sequence of events. "And this was, maybe, fifteen or twenty minutes before the rain started."

Megan's stare continued unabated. "Only five or ten minutes?" she asked.

"I was clear enough on the timeline," Elle replied, not backing down from the challenge. "Five minutes, ten tops.

We had a few words, and he left. Nothing more." She returned Megan's stare.

Cade shook his head and wrote a few notes. "Mom, I have to ask. What about you?"

Megan's eyes lingered on Elle for a moment more before she answered. "After dinner—or whatever we are calling what happened last night—I went up to my room with Stuart. As Elle so succinctly put it, we had a few words. He walked out. I never left my room, and I never saw him again. With the last words I spoke to him, I told Stuart to go to hell. Looks like he took it to heart."

Hendry slammed his hand against the counter. Angus bolted upright from his spot in the corner and sauntered from the room.

"You are an evil woman," he spat. "My son had his wicked ways, but he deserved far better than you. The entire Mac Uspaig clan deserves better than you."

"Life has taught me one thing," Megan replied. "We each get exactly what we deserve. Some just have to wait longer for it than others. Stuart is no different, and neither are you."

As Elle watched, several years' worth of barely hidden acrimony rose to the surface. Elle considered her options, then decided to step in. "This kind of animosity is only going to make this so much worse," she said aloud. "So, Megan was in her room," she added. "Hendry, where were you?"

"Where the hell else would I be?" he asked. "I was in my study with Daleroch. After Stuart's little theatrical performance last night, Leith and I had much to discuss. Neither of us left the room as I had no desire to see any of you. He didn't return to his own room until almost 3 a.m."

"Well, I can't answer for Lyle, but I was in our room from just after dinner until this morning," Caroline offered. "Lyle was so upset and needed to take a walk. He was only gone for maybe fifteen or twenty minutes."

From their seats around the kitchen island, each of the group turned to look at Lyle still standing at the window. Caroline laughed nervously. "Oh, really, it's not as if he came back covered in blood. He was barely gone for a few minutes."

"Lyle, answer for yourself," Hendry demanded with a note of resignation.

"Nothing to answer for, Dad," Lyle replied. "Just as Caroline said, I needed to walk off dinner. I took Coira and the rest down to the dock, then did a lap out the back and around to the west side of the house. I was nowhere near the terrace. I came in just as it started raining. After that I went up to our room and slept it off."

"Exactly as I said," Caroline added, sounding vindicated.

"And you're sure that everyone from off island actually got on the boat?" Elle asked.

"I'm certain," Lyle replied. "Miller was waiting with his ferry. They all got on board, and I saw them off. Should be easy enough to check with Miller if the police feel the need."

"That doesn't give us a whole lot to go on," Cade noted. "You guys were all over the place last night."

Elle thought of a follow-up question, but the conversation was interrupted by Detective Tanner. Leith was done with his interview, and now it was her turn.

"I think you've met most everyone here," Jonah noted as he offered Elle a seat at the dining room table. She glanced at the familiar faces and nodded.

"Hey Glen, Jeannie," Elle said.

"Looking good, Elle," Jeannie Pace replied. "Weren't expecting to see you this time around. I have to say it's been nice not seeing much of you lately." She smiled to underscore the lack of malice.

"Right back at you, Jeannie," Elle replied.

For his part, Glen Lewis just nodded. Warm expressions of welcome, Elle recalled, were not easy for Deputy Lewis.

"Okay, let's get this over with," Jonah began. "Let me start with the same thing I told Daleroch. Obviously, we are treating Mr. MacUspaig's death as a homicide. The crime scene team has done what they need at the house. Just please stay off the terrace for the rest of the day while they finish up out there." He paused. "So, Elle, we are going to do this in reverse," he continued. "Let's start with this morning, and then we will work back to last night. Got it?"

"Sounds good to me," she replied.

"Okay, take me through your actions this morning up until the moment we arrived," he requested. "And I think you know, don't leave anything out, no matter how trivial it may seem."

For the next ten minutes, Elle walked the officers through her routine from earlier in the day. Nothing new or unusual came to mind. Other than Stuart's body, there was nothing out of place on what have should been an otherwise very ordinary day.

"I have to ask again, did you notice anything unusual as you came up to the terrace?" Jonah asked.

"Nothing at all," Elle replied. "Angus, Lainie's hound, started howling when I came up the steps. I guess I was paying all my attention to him."

"Where was the dog?" Jonah said.

"I think he was in the bay window over in the library," Elle said, then thought for a moment. "It was only a split second before I saw Stuart on the ground."

"Anything there that needs mentioning?"

"No, just Stuart lying there," she said. "It took me a moment to take it all in, but nothing else seemed wrong with the picture. Just Stuart."

"Was there anything on the ground or near his body?" Jonah asked.

"Nothing," Elle replied. "I'm sorry this isn't more helpful. It was all so horribly off and perfectly normal at the exact same time. I guess I was expecting signs of a fight or a knocked over planter or bloody footprints or whatever."

"Did you touch anything?" Jonah continued.

"At first, I stood there, trying to fit the pieces together," she answered. "I bent over Stuart just as Lyle came out of the French doors from the library. He knelt down beside me and almost touched the handle of the dagger with his hand, but I slapped it away. I did feel Stuart's neck for a pulse, not that I imagined I'd find one." She shrugged. "I stayed with Stuart for a while until Leith called us all into the house. So, after I found him, I'm pretty sure that no one touched Stuart or anything else on the terrace."

"It's good you were thinking straight," Jeannie commented. "Our jobs would be much easier if there was one of you at every crime scene. Whenever something goes wrong, instinct tells most people to touch everything as often as possible. Half of our day is just sorting out what happened after the crime."

"Very true," Jonah agreed. "Elle, let's talk about last night. You've already told me what went on at dinner, and Mr. Daleroch confirmed that it was a circus. What did you do after the meal?"

"Well, not much," Elle said. "After half an hour or so, it was clear that everyone was just spinning their wheels. Stuart had his mind made up, and no one was going to change that. The group from off island decided to leave, so Lyle walked them down to the dock. I took that as an opportunity to duck out. I went straight back to the red cottage and got ready for bed."

"Anything else?" Jonah asked.

"Do you really need to ask?" Elle replied. "Maybe ten minutes later, there was a knock at my door. It was Stuart, and he was following up on an offer he had made before dinner."

"An offer?" Jeannie asked.

"We had a thing several years ago," Elle said. "Before he was married to Megan," she added quickly. "Let's just say he was looking for a nightcap. He came in, started getting comfortable and made a few very amateurish moves. Honestly, he was drunk. I figured he thought he was already single again."

"Did anything happen?" Jeannie asked with care.

"Nothing," Elle replied. "Last night was already a fiasco. I had no interest in making it any worse. So I sent him on his way. The whole conversation lasted all of fifteen minutes."

"Where did he go when he left?" Jonah asked.

"I didn't follow him, but he said that he had some decisions to make. He mentioned he was heading back to the house," she answered. "There's not anywhere to go on the island after dark."

"But you're not certain that he did?" Jeannie confirmed.

"Well, the front window on the cabin was open. A few minutes later I thought I heard him talking to someone else. It sounded like his voice was coming from the area near the terrace," she replied. "And before you ask, I have no idea what he was talking about, and I don't know who he was talking to. I never heard the other voice." Elle thought for a moment.

"Then, maybe five or ten minutes later the rain started. I woke up around 4 a.m. for a few minutes, and it was still raining."

"Elle, this is a good start," Jonah noted. "Is there anything else you can think of from this morning or last night that we should know about?"

Elle pondered the question. "There was one more thing," she noted. After another moment of thought, she reconsidered. "Make that two more things. First, when I got up this morning, the screen door on the cottage next to mine was left open," she said with confidence. "I am certain that I closed and latched it last night before dinner."

"Any chance it was Stuart?" Jeannie asked.

"I don't think so," Elle countered. "That's the second thing. I was thinking about the door, and that reminded me of something important. Before Stuart showed up, I was almost certain that I heard something next door. Maybe just a knocking around noise, maybe voices. In my head I thought it might be the wind, a loose shutter, I guess. Honestly, I just didn't care to find out what it was. I had completely written it off, but when I pair that with the screen door having been opened, my guess is someone was in there."

"Very good to know," Jonah replied. "I think it goes without saying that you need to stay out of there until we've had a look."

"Any chance I could get my laptop and notes?" Elle asked. "I use the white cottage for a writing setup. You can keep it shut tight as long as you need it."

"I'll walk you over before we leave, and you can grab the laptop," Jonah offered. "Everything else stays until we know what's going on."

"Thanks," she replied. "I've got the keys, which you can have until you're done with the place."

"Any other thoughts?" he asked.

"Jonah, I don't want to step on any toes," she said with a deep breath, keeping her eye on the young officer. "But I did have a few observations."

"Shoot," Jeannie replied.

"First," Elle began.

"First?" Jonah interrupted. "How many of these observations are there?"

"First," she repeated, "We all know that Stuart's body was wet from the storm. I'm fairly certain, however, he was killed before the rain began. If the rain had already started, he wouldn't have been standing around outside in his full kilt and jacket. That's a lot of very wet, very expensive wool. He would have, at the very least, been standing under the eave of the second-floor patio.

"Second," she continued, "I want to double down on what I said about Megan earlier."

"Want to fill us in?" Jeannie asked.

Jonah responded, "Elle feels Megan was in the dark about Stuart's visit to her cottage."

"That still doesn't clear her in Mr. MacUspaig's death," Jeannie noted. "Last night he announces he is divorcing her, and today he ends up dead. It's not a stretch."

"True," Elle replied, "but that was a surprise to everyone else but Megan. She made it pretty clear that divorce had been on the table for a while. It was just the timing that threw her. If she had wanted him dead, she could have found a dozen ways to do it before last night. And before anyone else knew that they might be splitting."

"I'd have to agree with you," Jonah admitted. "It doesn't clear her, but I think she just fell a few notches on the ladder of likely suspects. Of course, if you turn up dead in the morning,

I'll have to reevaluate that. Given the way she was looking at you, you'd be her next hit."

Jeannie laughed at the jab, while Elle ignore the remark.

"Finally," she concluded, "That dagger is one hell of a weapon. It has been on display in Hendry MacUspaig's study for decades."

"Mr. Daleroch noted that, too," Jeannie commented. "Someone went to a lot of trouble to go get it, bring it back downstairs and then kill MacUspaig."

"So we can agree that it was premeditated. There's no other reason to have retrieved the dagger," Elle offered. "Also, that weapon would be hard to hide. It's a good sixteen to eighteen inches from tip to pommel. I'm still not sure why Stuart would have turned his back on someone who popped up on the terrace holding that horrible thing."

"He must have known and trusted his killer," Jonah noted.

"I think it goes way beyond that," Elle replied. "I know you and trust you, Jonah. But if you show up out of the shadows after dark with a sixteen-inch knife in your hand, I'm not taking any chances."

Later that afternoon, the family gathered in the kitchen while the police wrapped up their interviews with Cade and Lainie. As his team collected their notes, Detective Tanner addressed the group.

"I know this has been a hard day for all of you," he began. "But I do have one more request. Until we have this sorted out, I need you all to stay in town. We may need to speak to you again."

"I can't speak for everyone," Lyle replied, "but Caroline and I have no other place to go. This is our home. We plan on staying right here."

"Cade and I will be staying as well," Megan added. "Until I hear differently, we are still welcome at Aldermire."

Leith stood and spoke to the officer. "On behalf of all of us, there is no other place we have to go at present," he said. "Despite the unpleasantry, I think we will all be staying at Aldermire for the next few days. And Miss Mackay, you are welcome to join us."

"Thank you, Leith. I wasn't planning on leaving just yet," Elle responded.

"I would ask, my dear, that you move to the main house," he added. "I know I would feel better if you were safely under this roof with the rest of us."

"You can take the guest room off the upstairs hall," Caroline offered. "Just give me a few minutes to find some sheets."

"Sounds like that has already been decided," Megan replied. "So very glad we decided to discuss this first. Whatever's best for the MacUspaigs, I guess."

Hendry MacUspaig, at last, spoke up. "For hundreds of years our clan has lived and died by the motto *'Perseverando.'* We will persevere; anything for the family."

"Or in Stuart's case, *'Quidlibet movet,'*" Megan added with a harsh cackle. Despite herself, Elle laughed out loud.

"You lost me," Jonah said.

"That's Latin-ish for 'Anything that moves,'" Elle noted.

6

The smoking room of the SL 100 Nereus was alive with foreign voices, a euphonious harmony of French, Greek, Russian, Italian and Queen's English. The laughter arising from the lively game of canasta, however, united the passengers with a common language.

From her customary chair beside the promenade windows, Mafalda Marchand regarded the New York skyline with a mix of awe and familiarity. True, this was her third transatlantic zeppelin voyage, but the sight of her adopted home never failed to fill her with wonder. She adjusted her signature monocle to better embrace the marvels before her.

Although it lacked the classical majesty of her Parisian birthplace, Manhattan was the future of civilization, she thought. As the airship drifted toward the new United Nations Headquarters, Mafalda caught her breath.

"There is truly no finer place to welcome 1939," she said aloud. "Celebrating New Year's Eve in New York City; how magical!" The feisty Brussels griffon in her lap barked as though in agreement.

"Hush, Heracles," she scolded. "Don't spoil the moment."

The skyline's spell broken, Mafalda considered each of her fellow passengers in turn. The Countess Menshikov appeared to be winning, she observed, if not at canasta then at the very least the contest for attention. The bright young couple from Oklahoma, the Browns if she remembered correctly, were at odds. Perhaps their honeymoon had taken an unfortunate turn.

The two questionable businessmen from Chicago were paying more attention to the countess than to their cardsmanship, Mafalda thought. The handsome young vicar from Strahmoor-on-Leeds, Jamison was his family name, completed the sextet. He was deep into the telling of a story that fascinated none but himself.

In the far corner, Major Brigadier General Farnesworth was sitting out for a hand. He alone seemed to find the noisy room a suitable spot for a quick nap. "You know, Heracles," Mafalda whispered to her pet, "perhaps he is as deaf as they say."

The porter, a slight yet swarthy Spaniard with dark eyes, brought her a second Mary Pickford. The pineapple juice and pomegranate-flavored grenadine blended with the heavenly rum into a fruity, delicious concoction. "Such an indulgence," Mafalda thought.

The porter continued making his rounds, next collecting the Major Brigadier General's empty sidecar glass. He jumped back as the elderly man's pipe fell unceremoniously from his sleeping hand, charred tobacco scattering across the floor.

He tried for a moment to rouse Farnesworth with a gentle shake. Instead of waking, the napping officer slumped forward in his chair. Mafalda sensed something was amiss and leapt to her feet.

"Young man, please step away immediately," she commanded. With only two strides she was at Farnesworth's side. A quick check of his wrist suggested no heartbeat; she could feel his body already beginning to cool.

While her instinct told her something was clearly wrong, her lightning-like intellect assessed the scene. His glass was empty, she noted. There was a black smudge on his left index finger that no pipe could account for. His reading glasses had mysteriously disappeared and, perhaps most vexingly, there were two pages torn from a Bible clearly visible in his jacket's breast pocket.

The salon's other occupants were starting to stir, their game of cards long forgotten. With a flourish, Mafalda extracted a handkerchief from her sleeve and carefully lifted the dead Farnesworth's glass. She sniffed and closed her eyes.

Even over the lingering scents of tobacco and more exotic herbs, Mafalda could detect a trace of burnt almonds. "Cyanide, no doubt," she thought to herself, "and perhaps an afterthought of ylang-ylang and lemon."

"My friends," she said aloud, commanding the attention of the room, "it appears there is a hint of murder in the air."

Elle groaned, closed the book and tossed it to the floor. Angus, lying beside her on the bed, took the movement as an opportunity to expose his belly. He nudged her leg with his nose in case she had missed the invitation. She surrendered and scratched him at her leisure. He returned the favor with a vigorous tail wag. He was soon asleep again.

"This is a best seller?" she asked the dog. Off the top of her head, she could list four things wrong with the narrative. Her thoughts ground to a halt as the cottage landline rang.

"Red cottage," Elle said, not quite sure why she responded in such an odd way.

"Hey, baby girl," her older sister answered. "Just wanted to give you one more call before dinner. Sophie and I are taking the twins out for pizza, maybe a movie. We'll be out for a few hours."

"Say hello to Soph for me and give the boys my love," Elle replied.

"You still doing okay?" Lana asked.

"Yeah, fine," she answered, "Jonah finished with us about an hour ago, and we're supposed to stay put until they wrap up whatever they are doing."

"You don't sound convinced they're doing enough," Lana prodded.

"It's something Stuart's brother said this morning," Elle replied. "This all just seems wrong. No better word for it, just 'wrong.' I trust Jonah, and he's a sharp guy, but shouldn't they be pulling the good cop, bad cop thing already? Let's get the lead out. Someone stabbed Stuart last night. Until the police figure this out, I'm probably sitting at dinner with whoever did it. Not doing great things for my appetite."

"Ellie, just stay busy and stay out of everyone's way. That includes Megan."

"She's not making it easy," Elle replied.

"Look at it from her point of view," Lana added. "She already has several reasons to dislike you. And before you say anything, no, they are not very good reasons. And now she's slapped with a surprise divorce, getting throw out of her home and waiting to find out who killed her bastard husband. She's had a lousy week. How about you cut her a break?"

"I hate it when you're right," Elle muttered.

"I thought you'd be used to that by now," Lana teased. "So how about you just keep your head down and find something to keep you busy."

"I'm working on it," Elle agreed. "In fact, I've been slogging through Bea's book."

"*Murder Over Manhattan*?" Lana asked.

"Yup," Elle replied. "Why didn't you warn me? This is straight-out awful."

"I got about halfway through it before I gave up on it," Lana said. "Why do you think I was so happy to lend it to you?"

"Four chapters in and I'm done," Elle noted. "This wasn't one of Bea's trickier plots."

"You figured it out?"

"Lana, I don't want to ruin it for you," Elle said.

"Don't worry, you know I hate mysteries," Lana replied. "Everything wraps up in 300 pages or less. Real life is never that easy. So, go ahead, impress me."

"Fine," Elle said, drawing a deep breath. "The countess killed him. The ylang-ylang and lemon are from the Chanel No. 5 she usually keeps in her tiny perfume atomizer. It's in her purse, and it's where she was hiding the cyanide."

"Hmmmm. Okay, but why kill the old guy?"

"Simple," Elle continued. "The countess is actually a Nazi spy trying to intercept a message between the Major Brigadier General and his secret connection."

"Who is..." Lana asked.

"Oh, that's the 'bright young' Miss Brown who is actually the famous propagandist Zelda Marron from the first chapter,"

Elle noted. "Marron can be translated to Brown in Spanish. She's also the one who took his glasses—to try to open the safe in the captain's quarters. Remember how bad her eyes were when she tried to read the luncheon menu?"

"And," Lana continued.

"The smudge is from the kitchen's ashbin where Farnesworth hid the codebook. The passage numbers circled on the Bible pages are the keys to the code," Elle concluded with more than a little self-satisfaction.

"Nicely done," Lana noted. "You're like a walking spoiler."

She paused for a moment, then added, "So what about dashing Father Jamison and the mobsters?"

"Easy," Elle answered. "Jamison is the eye candy. But he's in the clergy, which makes the whole thing a lot more taboo, yet still tasteful in a cozy mystery kind of way. Oh, and mobsters are *always* red herrings in her stories. It's Bea's shorthand for 'I look sketchy, so obviously I must be the killer.' She does it in every other book."

"For the rest of us, that could still be a heck of a puzzle," Lana responded. "Why are you so harsh on Bea's books? You've known her since high school. People love her stuff."

Elle thought for a few seconds. "You know," she said, "I don't have anything against her personally. It's just that the books are so, well, so sloppy."

"Sloppy how?"

"My top four from what I just read," Elle continued. "First, the Hindenburg disaster was in 1937. Transatlantic zeppelin service after that? Not gonna happen. Also, in 1938 the U.N. hadn't even formed, so they certainly didn't have a shiny new headquarters that early. Next, there's no such thing as a Major Brigadier General. You're either a Major General or a Brigadier

General, but not both. Last, the Bible was in his pocket. How could she possibly tell exactly two pages were missing?

"Okay, I know it's nitpicky, but this is history, this is what I do," she noted. "I mean, there's historical fiction, then there's creative license, then there's just sloppy. This is that last one."

"This, baby girl."

"This what?" Elle asked.

"This is why you don't get invited to parties."

Elle spent the hour before dinner collecting an overnight bag of toiletries and what few clean clothes she could find. She wasn't enthusiastic about the change of lodging, but Leith's suggestion made sense. If Stuart's death was not an isolated event, she'd fare better surrounded by the extended family, no matter how much some resented her presence. Given the choice between Megan and a potential murderer, Elle would choose Megan—by a slim margin.

As she zipped the bag, she heard a two-person conversation moving toward the cottage. Jonah's voice she had expected, although she couldn't quite place the other. Angus cocked his enormous ears forward, trying to locate the source of the interruption. Before Jonah could knock, she opened the door. She greeted him with his hand already raised, though the welcome was cut short. He stepped to one side to reveal Megan MacUspaig standing on the walkway behind him.

"Mrs. MacUspaig suggested she check the other cottage with me," he offered. "She felt she'd know best if anything had been moved or was missing."

"I have used it as a painting studio since moving to Roan," Megan added. "That is, until Stuart offered it to you for your little project."

Her sister's words in mind, Elle steered herself toward the high road. "I'm sorry for the inconvenience," she said. "It's been a huge help." Maybe a few small gestures of goodwill could slow, if not reverse, the steady escalation the two had managed these past few weeks.

"I have to be honest with you two," Jonah said. "This whole situation has been a challenge for my team. Looking at it from the outside, this place is a spider's web of connections overlapping connections."

"Welcome to Aldermire," Megan said without levity. "You, sir, have figured it out much sooner than most."

"Between the house, the estate, the games, marriages, and plenty else that I have yet to figure out, each of you is connected to the others in at least a dozen different ways," he continued. "With Stuart's huge reveal at dinner and all the fallout since, you all are literally one gun-toting Monsignor away from a telenovela." Jonah shook his head. "So has anyone here ever been held captive in a boathouse?" he asked. "Had a fist fight at a funeral? Maybe spent a year or more in a coma?"

"I do have an evil twin with amnesia," Megan offered.

"I'll be sure to put that in my report," he said with a smirk. He stopped to look at both women in turn.

"Look, I know you don't care for each other," he noted. "You've made that painfully clear. But Stuart meant something to each of you. That I believe. I also believe that Miss Mackay didn't have anything to do with his death. And I agree with her, Mrs. MacUspaig, that you probably didn't either."

At this admission, Megan gave Elle an odd look. The exact expression was difficult to read. Anger? Suspicion? Confusion? Perhaps all three? Elle was unsure.

"I need help from both of you," he continued. "Please, keep your eyes and ears open. If the physical evidence doesn't give us a clear direction, I'm going to need you to help me make sense of all of this. There are too many connections and too many opportunities for me to take a stab in the dark at this one." Then he quickly added, "I'm so sorry, horrible choice of words."

"We'll do what we can," Megan said, speaking for both women. Elle couldn't think of anything relevant to add and just nodded in agreement.

"This has been a hell of a day for the entire family," Jonah said. "I truly appreciate your help. How about we go check the other cottage?"

"The key is on the massive ring hanging there," Elle said, pointing to the hook beside her front door. "Leith gave me those to facilitate my research. I think I've got a key to every door on the island. The one you want is the key with the white paper tag. I usually keep the cottage locked because I can't afford to replace my laptop. If you need to keep the key, just take it off the ring. I think there's another one hanging in the rear entry hall at the big house."

"No longer," Megan interjected. "I checked before we walked over, and it's missing. Lainie last remembers seeing it maybe a week ago."

"Okay, that really needs to go into my report," Jonah noted. "Let's go take a quick look. Once I open the door, stay outside until I say otherwise. Understood?"

"Got it," Elle replied as she leashed Angus with his walking lead. Now it was Megan's turn to nod in agreement. They followed the detective outside to the white cottage door. As he began to try the key, Elle gave him an alarmed look.

"Don't worry, we've already dusted for prints," he commented. He opened the door and turned on his pocket flashlight to bolster the failing afternoon light.

"See anything out of place?" Jonah asked Megan. She glanced around the room and thought for a moment.

"Other than the laptop and paper stacks, nothing appears to be different or missing," she said. "Wait. The bed has changed. The pillows with the shams always go on top of the pillows with just cases. Someone has flipped those."

"You ever slept in the bed, Elle?" Jonah asked.

"Never needed to," she replied. "I've used it to spread out papers a few times, but I never touched the pillows."

"Anything else either of you see?"

Both women shook their heads. Nothing looked amiss.

"Elle, go ahead and grab your laptop and the charger," Jonah said. "Leave the papers for now. I'll get those cleared and back to you as soon as I can."

She stepped in and retrieved her computer. A second look around revealed nothing else out of place. She backed out slowly, trying to step in her own footsteps. In retrospect, she had no idea why she thought to do that. Jonah locked the cottage and took the key off the large ring of the estate's keys.

"Thank you, ladies," he concluded, then to Megan he added, "I need a minute alone with Miss Mackay. Do you mind?"

"It's fine. I need to be getting back to the big house," Megan replied. She took the hound dog's lead from Elle and walked off toward Aldermire without saying goodbye. Jonah opened the door to Elle's red cottage, and she followed him inside.

"Listen, I'd like help from both of you, but I'm really counting on you, Elle," he started. "You've got a good eye, and you're far enough outside the Aldermire ecosystem to be a bit more objective."

"Yeah, they keep reminding me just how outside I am."

"Use that to your advantage," he replied, "and to my advantage."

"Message received and understood," Elle said and gave him a mock salute. "Oh, and thanks for the vote of confidence. It's nice to know I'm not on the short list for who murdered Stuart."

He shrugged and blushed. "I think I know you well enough, and there was no reason for you to follow him all the way to the house before offing him."

"Jonah, why are you turning red?"

He sighed and shook his head. "You're going to hear about this sooner or later."

"Hear about what?" she asked.

"Your mother has spent most of the day on the phone with Sheriff Hopkirk," he said, testing the waters.

"Go on," Elle demanded with as much tact as she could muster.

"She was very clear that you couldn't have anything to do with Stuart's murder," he continued. "According to your mother, you are—and please understand that I'm only using her words—you are all talk and no action." He paused, waiting for a retort. When none came, he continued. "She felt that you aren't very strong at finishing what you start and that you certainly didn't have the gumption to kill someone."

"She better hope to God she's right about that," Elle said through clenched teeth. She held her breath, counted to ten, then counted to twenty and released a slow, deep exhale.

"You know, Elle, that's not a smart thing to say in front of a cop," he offered.

She considered his point. "I promise if I ever become a woman of action, I'll give you a call first," she said. "Mama would want everyone there for her big exit."

"Speaking of exits, I need to grab a lift back to Saint Andrews," Jonah replied. "I hope my team is still holding it for me at the dock."

"That's a heck of a swim," Elle said.

"Keep me in the loop," he said as he left the cottage.

"Will do," she replied and closed the door behind him.

Exhausted but not wanting to relive the disturbing dreams from earlier in the day, Elle lay back on the bed and stared at the ceiling. In her heart, she knew she should be focusing on her research. That was her path to the future she had planned. What happened to Stuart was a nightmare, but it would likely end up on someone else's shoulders.

And her mother. She sighed audibly. Elle knew Gavina was under her skin, and that's where her mother was most comfortable.

After a short pep talk, she resolved to make the move to the big house, where she would bury herself in her research. Her findings might offer the MacUspaigs some distraction and help them focus on the family's triumphs, not the tragedy.

As she rolled toward the edge of the bed, her eye caught a glimpse of something white on the floor. Lying beneath the chair where Stuart's sporran lay earlier was a four- or five-inch rectangle of white paper. It was not one of her own notes, and she was certain she hadn't seen it there before. She sat up, walked to the chair and picked up the slip.

In bold red block print, five words were handwritten on the scrap: "You have broken the fifth."

7

To all life thou givest—to both great and small;
In all life thou livest, the true life of all;
We blossom and flourish as leaves on the tree,
And wither and perish—but naught changeth thee.

— Walter Chalmers Smith,
Immortal, Invisible, God Only Wise

Elle woke the next morning in a cavernous canopied bed. The transition from sparse cottage to luxurious guest room at the grand house was a welcome one. She considered spending the day in bed; perhaps no one would notice if she barricaded herself in with pillows.

Since Stuart's death, the house and the family had taken agitated turns. The group was restless and on edge. Elle knew they were each facing an unknown future, and their uncertainty was churning into aggravation. A day or two of isolation, she conceded, might be a change for the better.

She covered her head with the silk duvet, a meager defense against the morning light encroaching through the large windows. Elle reconsidered her options when the faint smell of cooking bacon rose from the kitchen below. It was incentive enough to rouse her from her feathered retreat. Still, she took her time dressing. She was hungry, but the thought of a full day spent with the remaining MacUspaigs didn't foster her appetite.

As she made her way down the stairs and toward the kitchen, she could hear two voices. It was Lyle and Caroline, of that she was sure. They were arguing, albeit politely and early.

"Who gives a damn about the gardens or whatever the hell Coira has planned," she heard Lyle say in a barely hushed tone. "This house is what's important."

"Honey, you're not looking at the big picture," Caroline responded. "The house isn't going to keep itself up. We need to..." Feeling guilty for eavesdropping, Elle pushed her way through the swinging servants' door and into the dining room before Caroline could finish.

"Good morning," she said, a touch louder than she had planned. "I could smell breakfast all the way upstairs and couldn't stay put." She hoped she sounded causal and uninterested in what might have been said. In retrospect, she was certain it came across as rehearsed.

Caroline froze mid-sentence. Elle could see that, for a brief moment, the young Mrs. MacUspaig was rewinding their conversation in her head. What had she said? What should she have not said? Her face simply broke with a generous smile.

"Elle, I didn't expect to see you up so early! How did you sleep?"

"Like a baby; that bed is divine." She resolved to dial back the enthusiasm.

A patter of padded footsteps signaled Angus' arrival at her feet. Over the past two days, the hound had learned to recognize and appreciate the newest houseguest. To his apparent delight, he had found an endless source of ear scratches and belly rubs.

"Don't mind us," Lyle added. "We're trying to make heads or tails of what to do next. Stuart's death has left so many things up in the air. It feels like we are all just chasing our tails."

Elle's instincts had been right. Where there was bacon, there was breakfast. As she worked her way through the line of dishes, the couple at the table sat silently. Both MacUspaigs were fidgety. Elle felt her presence was making them nervous. While she filled her plate with bacon, scrambled eggs, fruit, dry toast and more bacon, she considered the pair's reflection in the decorative mirror over the buffet.

In many ways, Lyle was a younger version of Stuart. Although born just over twenty years apart, the brothers shared a similar presence, a similar bearing. Lyle's hair tended toward a darker red, and he had yet to develop the early gray common to most MacUspaig men. The short-cropped beard and mustache gave him a more serious demeanor, although his gawky movements belied a young man who had not yet grown into his own body. *In time, he might develop the charm that made Stuart so irresistible,* she thought, *but he needs to find the confidence to back it up.*

Caroline was another easy read. In her late twenties, she was young and engaging, but she had yet to find a channel for her nervous energy. She was shorter than her husband by eight or nine inches and didn't share his natural athleticism.

Elle took a seat across from the younger woman. "I can't imagine what you two are going through right now." Elle felt a sincere sympathy for them both. "I'd be spinning in circles if I were in your shoes."

Sometime earlier in the month, Caroline had begun wearing dark-rimmed glasses. Elle assumed they were intended to give her an added note of seriousness, which could work if she were the "smart and silent" type. No such luck.

"Elle, you've been here for weeks, and I love spending time hearing about your research," she said. "But for the life of me, I don't think I know the first thing about you. There is nowhere any of us need to be this morning, so tell me all about yourself."

The request caught Elle off guard. She reached down to pet the sleeping hound wrapped around her feet, stalling for a moment to collect her thoughts. Before she could answer, Caroline was tapping her fingers against her juice glass with a fidgety rhythm. In fact, Elle couldn't remember a time when Caroline wasn't tapping her foot, talking with her hands or twirling a strand of long, processed blond hair around a finger.

"I don't know that there's much to tell," she replied. "I grew up here in Saint Andrews with my sister. Married and divorced with no kids."

"So is your family originally from the Wilmington area?" Caroline asked.

"Well, Wilmington for as long as I've been alive. My parents were from Scotland. So is my older sister. They arrived in the Carolinas just before I was born. My sister and my mother still live on Eagle Island."

"I adore Saint Andrews," Caroline chirped. "I grew up in Wilmington proper, and a trip to the island was always a treat for us as children."

"We felt the same way about a trip downtown," Elle added with a laugh.

"My family has been in Wilmington since forever," Caroline continued. "My father owned Buchanan's Mill, and before him his father and grandfather back some five generations."

A light bulb went off in Elle's mind. "Buchanan? Are you related to Dr. Buchanan-Berman?"

"Oh, I thought you already knew that," she replied. "Coira is my father's oldest sister. In fact, Aunt Coira introduced me to Lyle at a dinner here on Roan not four years ago."

Lyle cut her off with a smile. "And the rest is history."

"Not so fast," Caroline added. To Elle she confided, "I just love telling this story. I was home from graduate school for the summer, and Aunt Coira gave me a job managing the books for her practice. She invited me out to Aldermire for the evening. I had been here several times when I was a girl, but not since then. I met Lyle at dinner, and it was love at first sight!"

Lyle's expression suggested it might have been second or third sight for him. He leaned back in his chair and looked away. Elle was sure he had heard the story before and had no interest in hearing it again.

"He was so dashing and handsome, and then I found out he was one of the MacUspaigs," she gushed. "I just knew we were meant to be together forever. We started dating immediately. His father was just thrilled; Hendry said I was the perfect girl for him. Not that Hendry still seems to think so. I hate to admit it, but the old grouch was right, and we married two years ago. We were going to do a big wedding, but Stuart and Megan really stole our thunder the year before."

At the mention of Stuart's name, Lyle's eyes snapped back to Elle and his wife. Elle realized that the reality of his brother's death was still sinking in.

Elle changed the subject. "This whole thing must have been a nasty shock," she probed.

"When is death not a shock?" Lyle replied. "But Stuart and I might as well have been from different generations. While I was growing up here at Aldermire, he was out living his life. The house was his, but he never seemed happy here. He'd leave on some adventure. Then Dad would try to reel him in, but it never took. He didn't really come back on a permanent basis until he married Megan. That was, what, three years ago."

"And even then, he wasn't around that much," Caroline added.

"I will certainly miss him," Lyle continued. "Honestly, the difference in years made him less of a brother to me and more of an uncle who would drop in every so often. When he brought Megan and Cade to live on Roan, we had the chance to get to know each other better."

"That must have been rough," Elle said. "Fortunately for me, growing up I was only three years behind my sister Alana. And for girls, a three-year difference is nothing. I can't imagine that sort of gap."

"He was a good enough guy. It's just that every time he'd show up, he and Dad would end up at odds," he said. "It was like clockwork. Stuart would arrive, two days later they'd be arguing and then one or the other would storm off. Eventually Stuart would leave, only to show up later and start the whole damned thing over again."

"I don't mean to pry," Elle said with care, "but with everything so up in the air right now, do you both have any idea what your options are? I wasn't sure if you had spoken to Leith or Hendry."

Lyle looked at Caroline with a puzzled stare while Caroline made small piles of the eggs left on her plate. "Well, we are thinking about that today," he replied. "Coira and the Mac Farlanes are coming over to Roan in a few minutes. The five of us will sit down with Leith to see what, if anything, can be done about the house."

"And Aunt Coira's foundation," Caroline added quickly.

"And Coira's foundation," he repeated without emotion. "I hope that conversation will give us a little direction or, at least, let us know what our options are."

"Afterwards some of us are going into Wilmington," Caroline said. "Probably just Cade and the girls. Leith suggested we maybe see a movie; anything to get out of this house for a few hours. I would love it if you'd join us."

"Sounds like a nice change of scenery, but I'm going to sort through my notes," Elle replied. "The past two days have taken me off track, academically speaking. I could use the quiet time to refocus on my work."

"If you change your mind, we'd welcome one more."

As Elle cleared her plate she mapped out the rest of her day. Despite the allure of her oversized bed, she needed time to focus on her research. A quick trip up the back servants' stairs brought her to the second floor.

As she wound her way through the maze of hallways, bedrooms, guestrooms and parlors, Elle gave herself time to study the dozens of oil portraits lining the halls. In each, the eras changed; the clothing, hairstyles and even artistic skills varied from one portrait to the next. In the faces, however, she saw a common thread. It was more than the broad shoulders, the various shades of red hair and the square, regal jaws shared by most of the men and women depicted.

"It's the sense of pride," Elle concluded. In each she saw a nobility and hint of fire common to the members of Clan MacUspaig. Each was proud to call the clan, the home and the island as his or her own. It was unmistakable.

As she obsessed over the delicate brushwork in a formal portrait of Carolyn McClellan MacUspaig (born 1843), she thought she heard, if only for a second, the tune of "Taladh Chriosda", an old Scottish hymn popular during the Christmas season. Through the melody she could make out the faint words, all in the original Scottish Gaelic, echoing from one of the rooms nearby. According to her mother, the verse was a parent's blessing on a child fairer than the sun.

B' e sin sgeula binn nam beannachd,
Mu'n aoidh a rinn tearnadh gu talamh,
Cha'n ioghnadh mi 'bhi muirneach, geanail.
Is gile na ghrian mo leanamh.

Beguiled, she followed the sound of the choral voices. With some twenty verses to go, she didn't feel the need to rush.

The music led her to the massive door of Hendry Mac Uspaig's study. Over the past six weeks, she had walked past this room many times. She had not, however, been invited in. The door was ajar, so she seized the opportunity to see inside.

"Young lady, have you always been a Mackay?" a gravelly voice asked from within the sanctuary.

Elle paused, both mystified and amused by the old man's brusque welcome.

"No, that's my married name," she replied at the door. "I'm divorced now, but the name seems to have stuck. I was born a Cunningham."

"Ah, that's right. You're one of Vee's daughters," Hendry continued. "Don't stand there like a damned fool. Either come in or not, I don't care either way."

She entered the patriarch's study, a dark, dense room filled with books and overstuffed chairs. The far wall was a massive stone fireplace and a single tall window. Despite the warmth of the morning sun, a fire raged behind an elaborate iron grill. The intricate metalwork depicted the Clan MacUspaig crest, a large hand holding a Huguenot cross.

"You look surprised, loitering there with your mouth agape," he said. "I know every footfall in this house. For nearly eighty years it has been my home and castle. Don't think I don't recognize the footsteps of a strange woman in my domain."

The elder MacUspaig pointed to a chair opposite him, a motion Elle took as an invitation to sit. As she made her way across to the room, he used a small remote control to turn off the room's hidden sound system.

"Good folk, the Cunninghams," Hendry said as he looked past her and out the room's sole window. "Always industrious and honest. My first supervisor was a Cunningham from a local family. Andrew Cunningham, if my fading memory still serves me well. One of your kin?"

"Likely not," Elle replied. "My line is a more recent arrival. Mom and Dad both came over from Ayr just before I was born."

"Aye," he chuckled. "A new family from the old country." He returned his gaze to her as though he was looking at her for the first time. "We always like to think of ourselves as coming from old stock. How easily we forget that the oldest stock is still an ocean away."

"As far as the States are concerned, your family is certainly old stock," Elle noted. "Thus far I've reviewed family records back past the early 1700s. That's some 300 years."

"Just a bit longer than that," Hendry said. "My several times great grandfather and grandmother came over on the Henry & Francis in 1685. It was largely a Reformed Presbyterian group, but despite being Reformed Protestants my ancestors were accepted for passage. They eventually settled near here when the

Cape Fear River was still a major port for the shipping trades. Made enough to secure Roan Island for generations to come."

"That is all new information for me," Elle noted, her enthusiasm for the conversation beginning to rise. "I'd love to know more about the start of the MacUspaigs in the Americas. Any documents you have on that period would be invaluable for my research."

"Aye, your research," he replied. In an instant, his mood darkened. For a moment, he looked every one of his seventy-eight years. His once red hair turned white and wispy in the flickering firelight, and the soft glow exaggerated the stoop of his once broad shoulders.

"I feel I should be honest with you," he said with great concern in his voice. "You haven't had the warmest welcome from me. It may be undeserved, but that's the way it's been.

"You may find great comfort in your work, but for one such as me, it can only bring pain," he noted. "Your presence here underscores the truth I have already begun to accept: as a clan, the MacUspaig family may be drawing to a close. When I think back over the years, I can still see the faces of my father, his brothers, my cousins and my own brothers. All MacUspaigs by name and birth and now all gone, save me and my boys... my boy. Whoever thought that our proud family history could sputter out here on the same island on which we have prospered for centuries?"

"I know that the family line is very important to you," Elle offered. "I didn't want to cause you any undue discomfort. If anything, I wanted to record the clan's rich tradition, should anything happen." She caught her words as she said them.

"Aye, should anything happen," he repeated. "And happened it has. With Stuart's death, my family—reaching back countless generations—and our home rest solely on the shoulders of Lyle. May he be a better guardian of that legacy than his brother."

"Lyle and Caroline are still newlyweds," Elle said with encouragement. "I can't imagine they won't have children. Several of them, if I'm guessing right."

"Between you, me and these four walls, I never cared a lick for that woman," Hendry admitted without rancor. "She's a thinker and an opportunist, but as a wife she'll serve her purpose."

"You don't sound impressed," she observed.

"I've seen the wives come and go," he said. "Caroline is the woman of the house for now. Megan served briefly in the role, and Quacey before her. And before her my own dear Catheryn, God rest her soul. To an old man like me, they are all the same."

At the mention of Stuart's first wife, Elle's ears pricked. Leith Daleroch's oldest daughter and Lainie's older sister, Quacey was rarely mentioned at Aldermire. She and Stuart had married early, and she had died before Elle and Stuart had reconnected.

"In all the years I knew Stuart, he rarely mentioned Quacey by name," Elle said. "I can't remember even seeing a picture of her here at Aldermire. Was there a story to be told?"

"Aye, but not a happy one," he admitted. He thought for a minute before rising from the chair and walking to the study window. "Stuart and Quacey Daleroch were high school sweethearts. She was a simple girl, but my damned fool son was smitten. They married soon after graduation and hoped to start a family. I knew that Stuart was the future of Clan Mac Uspaig. At the time he was my only son, so Catheryn and I granted him full ownership of the house and island. It was our wedding gift to them both.

"But she was an ungrateful girl. Not three years after they married, Stuart was in Virginia competing at the Highland games up north. One morning, the daft girl said she was taking the skiff over to Wilmington to post a few letters. Then she just up and left. No note and no trace of her, just the boat run aground over near Old Town. We spent a month searching every corner of the Cape Fear basin, but we turned not even a trace of her passing."

"That must have been horrible for Stuart," Elle said. "I can't imagine not knowing where she'd gone. Or why."

"Oh, I think we know the 'why,'" he replied. "She had it in her mind she'd be the lady of the manor. Expected to be waited on hand and foot. She never understood that a MacUspaig works for what the world provides. It's our way. Life on Roan proved to be no bed of roses, so she sought another life somewhere else."

"How did the rest of the family take it?" Elle asked.

"Stuart and Leith were out of their heads with worry," he recalled. "Leith was already a widower by then, and he and Lainie had come to live on Roan, although she wasn't even ten at the time. Catheryn, my late wife, was on the island as well when Quacey left. Catheryn organized search parties, held vigils for the girl. Over time the searching slowed, and the fliers came down. Later that year, Lyle surprised us all, although Catheryn died during his birth. Soon, time marshalled on and the girl was forgotten by most."

Hendry paused and looked out the window toward the ground below.

"I see the vultures have arrived," he said with a hint of bile. "Come to pick over the corpse of Aldermire before it's even grown cold." He paused again and muttered under his breath, "The old house may surprise them still."

8

It was cold and barren. It was no longer the view that I remembered. The sunshine of her presence was far from me. The charm of her voice no longer murmured in my ear.

— Wilkie Collins, *The Woman in White*

Echoing up from the foyer, Caroline and Lyle's voices rose, welcoming Coira to their home. Red and Anne MacFarlane soon added their good-natured hellos. From where she stood just inside an upstairs archway, Elle stayed out of sight until the conversation faded into the library. In half a dozen steps, she was across the grand staircase landing and into the luxury of her guest room.

In the sudden quiet, she stood motionless in the center of the room. With the thick oaken door closed, the house and its inhabitants disappeared into the distance. Muffled voices faded away, and Elle imagined herself alone in the world. Although she had enjoyed an excellent night's sleep, the warmth, silence and stillness sapped her energy. She stacked several pillows against the headboard and made herself comfortable.

She reached for her notepad on the bedside table and reviewed her remarkably civil conversation with the MacUspaig patriarch. A few notes helped memorialize the stories he told of the earliest clan members in what was then the American colonies. They served as one bookend of the history she was going to write. She wrote a quick reminder to press Hendry for further information or, better yet, documentation on these seventeenth and eighteenth century MacUspaigs.

More interesting to her were the stories of the current generation. She had heard of Quacey in conversation, but the history of the first Mrs. Stuart MacUspaig had remained a mystery. That is, until today.

While the new information wasn't entirely a revelation, it did provide her with a deeper understanding of the family's patriarch and how he related to the members of his household. Stuart's lack of affection for Aldermire, Lyle's need to please, even Leith's endless devotion to the old estate—they each made more sense through the lens of Quacey's disappearance.

Lying back on the forgiving wall of feather pillows, Elle let her mind wander. Two days ago she had been sorting grave rubbings. She had been collating dates and names, cross-checking family members and relationships. Her tumultuous life had achieved a degree of serenity. She was working, she was grounded, and she was happy.

With Stuart's death, she worried she could lose her focus. She couldn't afford to risk the momentum she had worked so hard for. Losing this tenuous lifeline scared Elle more than she was willing to admit. The research project was a step, and an important one, to finding her way back to the old Elle, to the before-the-divorce Elle.

"Stuart might be gone, but I am still in control," she said aloud. Elle resolved to have the final say on how her time at

Aldermire propelled her forward. She had earned a few days to refocus and settle into this new normal.

In her mind, Stuart was still the heart of the problem. If Jonah couldn't figure exactly what had happened, Elle worried, the questions left unresolved would be an unending distraction. She needed answers. She needed closure. And the thought of sleeping in this house with his killer did nothing to brighten her mood.

The last of the morning sun flooded in through the tall windows, bathing her in a warm glow that contrasted with the crisp coolness of the sheets. Despite the mid-morning hour, Elle soon felt herself floating between sleeping and waking.

As she slept, she dreamt. She walked through the twisting halls of Aldermire, the soft melody of "Abide with Me" floating just beyond her hearing. There were no doors to open and no other halls to explore, so she continued forward past an endless army of MacUspaig portraits. The subject of each painting turned in silence as she passed. They were watching her, judging her, and she knew it.

The hall snaked on for what felt like miles, and the paintings began to openly discuss Elle's presence with one another. Although their conversations grew louder, she heard a sweet voice in the distance. It was pure and light, yet it somehow made itself heard above the din. Elle could just make out the words that accompanied the hymn:

Hold Thou Thy cross before my closing eyes;
Shine through the gloom and point me to the skies.
Heaven's morning breaks, and earth's vain shadows flee;
In life, in death, O Lord, abide with me.

As the voice sang the final words, Elle could see its source in the distance. A young woman, clothed in white and yellow, was moving slowly down the hallway just ahead of her. No matter her speed, Elle found she couldn't reach the woman. She called out, but the apparition refused to answer. Instead it continued on its ethereal path. All too soon, the woman in white disappeared around a distant corner, and when Elle reached the turn, the woman was gone.

Elle woke feeling restless. The bedside clock noted that it was still before lunch, so her nap hadn't taken more than an hour. With most of the family gone for the afternoon, she had the ideal chance to spread out her research in the library and formulate a new perspective on what she had so far collected.

After a five-minute search, she realized that her massive ring of keys and her most recent notepads were still at the red cottage. Hoping to sidestep any conversation with the downstairs guests, Elle made her way to the back servants' stairs. In the kitchen she grabbed the last two pieces of bacon still sitting out from breakfast, and she slipped out the back door.

Her efforts misfired. Standing just outside the servants' door to the grand terrace, Dr. Coira Buchanan-Berman and both MacFarlanes were deep in conversation. Anne MacFarlane jumped as Elle opened the door, and she blushed as she stumbled through a greeting.

"Miss Mackay, we didn't know you were still at Aldermire," she said in a rush of words. Coira maintained her unflappable air of composure, extending Elle a warm handshake in welcome.

"So very delightful to see you again," the doctor said. "I know this has been simply a nightmare for everyone here on Roan, but I hope the incident with Stuart hasn't distracted you from your work. History waits for no man, or woman as the case may be."

Elle accepted the handshake and thanked the trio for the generous reception. "In fact, I was just walking to my writing space to collect a few notes," Elle continued. "Stuart's murder has turned Aldermire upside down, and I need to keep my focus."

At the mention of murder, Anne touched her own throat and gave an audible gasp. Over the past two days, Elle had heard of Stuart's passing, his death, his untimely accident, his incident and his misfortune. It was now time to call it what it clearly was: murder. It appeared that Coira agreed.

"Oh, Anne," Dr. Buchanan-Berman chided, "what else should she call it? Stuart died, and not at his own hand. I'd think it would be something to titillate that morbid little granddaughter of yours. The family crypt isn't the only bloody spectacle on Roan Island."

Red stepped to his wife's defense. "Coira, it's been a shock for us all," he said. "In three centuries, there's never been a murder at Aldermire."

"Not one that we know of," Coira replied.

Anne shook her head. "Coira, please."

"Why don't you two run down to the docks," the doctor suggested. "I need a word with Miss Mackay about her research. And Anne, when you get to the docks, take the little walk to the left. It's a beautiful view of the river, and it will give you a chance to collect your breath. I'll be along in a few minutes. Have Miller wait for me, please."

Red took Anne by the arm and walked her down the path, past the spot where Stuart's body once lay and across the lawn to the docks. Coira turned to Elle with an inviting smile.

"Such a delight to run into you this morning," she began, "and so unexpected. I hope you've been delving deep into the MacUspaig family history."

"Deeper every day," Elle replied. "This morning alone I've gotten a little firsthand history from Lyle, Caroline and Hendry. In my work I've found that people tend to open up after a tragedy. It makes them nostalgic, sometimes remorseful, and they want to talk about it."

"Very true," Coira said, "and quite insightful. So, what stories did they regale you with today?"

"Caroline told me about her first meeting with Lyle and how they became a couple," Elle noted. "I had no idea she was your niece."

Coira laughed. "Ah, little Carrie. She has always been a bundle of nervous energy. She loves to tell a tale or two."

"She mentioned that when they met it was love at first sight," Elle continued.

"Oh, it was love at first site," Coira replied. "But it wasn't Lyle she fell for."

"Really? Then who?"

"Not 'who,' but rather 'what.' She fell in love with Aldermire—the history, the grandeur, the opulence. Lyle has always been simply a means to an end. I don't mean to be crass about my own kin, but it's an accepted fact here on Roan."

"That can't be easy for Lyle," Elle replied.

"Nothing is easy for Lyle," Coira continued. "When Catheryn died giving birth, he became an afterthought. As a result, Lyle has always lived in his brother's shadow. Stuart had the charm, the house, the tragic backstory, and a twenty-year head start."

Elle raised her hand to slow the doctor's words. "I had heard that Catheryn died when Lyle was born," she noted, "but why is she not buried in the family crypt? According to everything I've read, the crypt hadn't been opened for decades before we started our research."

Coria tilted her head. "That's an odd tale from a family history filled with odd tales. Her final will demanded that she be buried with her family, the McCullens, in the clan plot outside of Durham. Hendry never fought the request. I can only imagine that she didn't relish the idea of spending eternity next to that miserable man. All hellfire and damnation. It must have been insufferable."

"I can't imagine that Caroline knew what she was marrying into," Elle said.

"And don't waste any sympathy on Carrie. She is a material girl, as I think they are called now. She grew up with a silver spoon in her mouth. Sadly, her father—my brother—lost everything in real estate some fifteen years ago, and Caroline has spent her youth clawing her way back to the top."

"Have you always known the MacUspaigs?" If Coira was willing to talk, Elle was willing to ask.

"Oh, for decades," she replied. "The Buchanans and Mac Uspaigs were the first heart of Saint Andrews before Hendry's people moved here to Aldermire. Growing up I would babysit for Stuart, Quacey and their families whenever needed. When I came home after graduate school, I got involved with Hendry's precious gardens and the games on Eagle Island. It's been that way ever since. Oh, listen to me ramble on," Coira chided herself. "So what did Hendry have to say about all this?"

"Nothing at all," Elle replied. "He told me about poor Quacey. I had heard her name before, but I never knew the whole story."

"I don't think any of us know the whole story. You may not be aware, but Stuart was investigated thoroughly after she disappeared. In town, the prattle was that Quacey was the one who hated living at Aldermire, but in reality I know they both found married life a poor fit. It's not uncommon for such a young couple. They were living with his family, and they had very little direction. He was burdened with the running of Aldermire. A few drinking problems, several failed pregnancies, countless rumored affairs and more than one recriminating argument later, there were bound to be problems."

"Was Stuart ever charged?" Elle asked.

"Well, at the time there was no body, no crime and nothing to charge him with," Coira replied. "Quacey has never turned up, alive or dead. And he had a good, if not rock solid, alibi for the morning she disappeared. Several of us were up near Richmond for a few weeks in advance of the Old Colony Games. In fact, I had dinner with him the night before. Of course, it's possible he drove down, boated over to Aldermire, did something regretful, then returned to his hotel. But I doubt it.

"My apologies, Elle. I got sidetracked, dredging up all that unfortunate family history. The history I need to speak with you about is both much more distant and much more current."

"What do you need to know?" Elle asked.

"Well, the stark reality is that now Stuart is dead, Aldermire may very well flourish on Roan Island," she replied. "Yes, it sounds terribly opportunistic, I know, but it's a simple truth. I'd like to put all the history you've been collecting and collating to good use."

Elle shrugged. "I think my book is good enough use."

"Oh, I mean no offense, my dear. Let me rephrase that. I'd like to put that fascinating history to another good use; this time for the good of us all."

"Go on."

"We both know the crucial role Roan Island played in the history of the region, from shipping and smuggling to timber and agriculture," Coira continued. "I'd like to work with you to fast track Aldermire a spot on the national or state Register of Historic Places. I'll pay you for your work, and I'll cover any fees or costs we may accrue."

"Given the history of the island and the architecture of the house and outbuildings, it shouldn't be an uphill battle," Elle replied. "I'm not an expert in this area, but I can help pull the information together."

"I know Mr. Daleroch still needs to determine who is the current owner of Aldermire, but I think I've gotten the go-ahead from the most likely candidates. It may not be a quick process, but this sort of designation could prevent Roan from being further developed. It might be my one long-term solution toward preserving the history of the estate."

The doctor produced a business card from her jacket pocket and handed it to Elle. "I'll be in touch. Mustn't keep the MacFarlanes waiting any longer."

As Elle watched her stride across the lawn, the first storm winds began to blow. Just south of the island, dark clouds were gathering for the second time in a week. Fearing another heavy rain, Elle picked up her pace and turned toward the red cottage.

The room was still small and cluttered. Her notes and stacks of research materials were exactly as Elle had left them. She found the familiar chaos comforting. This was her world, she thought, the lives and deaths of those long since departed.

She considered staying for a while. If Caroline, Megan and the others took the boat to Saint Andrews, certainly no one would miss her for a few hours. As quickly as the thought came, it vanished with the first few drops of rain against the cottage windows.

Anticipating a downpour, Elle grabbed two piles of notes on the early nineteenth century MacUspaigs and wrapped them in an unused sheet of tracing paper. If she had to be trapped at Aldermire, perhaps she could pick Hendry's brain over some of the murkier corners of the family history. She pocketed two small notebooks and the chunky ring of estate keys before sprinting along the path back to the main house.

The rain began to fall in earnest as she vaulted through the French doors into the library. She dropped her bundled notes on a tapestry-covered chair by the bay window and brushed the loose water from her shoulders and hair.

"You certainly escaped the worst of it," a voice said, startling Elle. She followed Leith's familiar chuckle to the overstuffed chair closest to the empty fireplace. He sat cross-legged and wrapped in a warm robe, a large volume from the countless library shelves resting on his lap. Angus rested motionless at his feet.

"You look entirely too comfortable," she replied with a smile.

"My favorite chair, my favorite robe and my favorite book. What better way to spend a rainy day?"

"It suits you," Elle said. "Were you in the meeting with Coira and the rest?"

"Only for a few minutes," he replied. "They have far too many questions, and I have far too few answers. Everyone is scrambling for a piece of Aldermire. Estate matters have not always been a strength of mine, and this one is a mess." He paused to rub his eyes. "I'll worry about answers tomorrow. Today is for the written word and quiet reflection."

"What are you reading?"

"An endless source of inspiration," he said, patting the large book. "The collected tragedies of William Shakespeare. Although I haven't yet settled on the exact work. Perhaps 'King Lear' or 'Othello.' Perhaps 'Titus Andronicus.' One has so many sad stories from which to choose."

"I'd think you'd have had enough sad stories for a while," she commented. "The collective mood here seems to be in free fall."

"That, my dear, is the nature of family," he replied. "They can be the source of great joy or unbearable despair, but they make life worth living."

"You and Hendry share a great devotion to family," Elle noted.

"An apt observation, to an extent. I have always put my heart into the importance of family. Hendry is a great believer in the importance of *the* family. On paper, it seems an arbitrary distinction. To my dear friend, the true value of a life comes from the name, the estate, the clan, the legacy—in short, the family. Stuart's death has hit him very, very hard. Stuart was his chosen son, the golden boy, the family's path to a future generation. With Stuart gone, that path has narrowed. The loss of Lyle would be a fate worse than death for Hendry. It would mean the death of the entire Clan MacUspaig. Hendry knows it, and he fears it."

"Have you spoken to him about Stuart's death?" she asked.

"I have tried, but he keeps retreating back into his cocoon. He wraps himself in the comfort of the MacUspaig legacy like a protective blanket. I urged him to come meet with Lyle, Coira and the rest. He'd have none of it. His only concern is ensuring that the estate passes to his younger son and that his line carries on. He couldn't care less about Caroline, Megan, Cade or the rest. As long as Lyle follows him as lord of Aldermire, his life was well lived."

"I spoke to him earlier this morning," Elle noted. "He told me about Stuart and Quacey. I had heard her name, but I didn't know the whole story."

"I don't think we will ever know the whole story," Leith said, bowing his head.

"I am so very sorry for your loss," she said. "I can't imagine what that must be like."

"It's something that every parent dreads," he said. He removed his glasses and rubbed his eyes. "The death of a child puts so many things into stark perspective. And before you ask, I do consider it a death. She was a source of pure hope and love, and I know in my heart that the wellspring is forever gone.

"To your comment earlier about family, unlike Hendry I don't place the importance on the clan or the legacy. A son or daughter, to me they are the same. They are someone to love and to cherish. A child is someone who will carry on, not a name, but a sense of family and what it means to belong.

"To a certain degree, I understand Hendry's grief and his sudden notice of Lyle," he continued. "When my wife died not long after Lainie was born, it left just me and my girls. Whether they stayed Dalerochs or married and became MacUspaigs, Smiths or Joneses, they were my daughters and they were loved."

"You chose beautiful names for your girls," Elle said, unsure if anything she could say could comfort her friend.

"When Quacey was born, she had the sweetest, roundest face." He laughed at the memory.

"Isn't that traditionally a boy's name?" she asked.

"It certainly is," he said with a beaming smile. "My wife had been certain we were expecting a boy. I don't know why. Add that to her round face and we came up with Quacey, or moonlight."

"I see a theme," Elle replied. "Isn't Lainie an Old English word for shining or bright?"

"It's close enough," he said. "And it is an apt name. Since Quacey's death, Lainie has been the light of my life. When her sister disappeared, Lainie took it very hard. I think she was unsure *why* Quacey left, why she had abandoned her. Lainie was still so young then. I don't know that she's ever gotten over that loss. She sleeps with a photo of her on her nightstand, looking as she'll always remember her. And now, after all these years, tragedy has returned to Aldermire. To quote Shakespeare, 'Chaos is come again.' And with it, I fear, the pain of loss."

As the pair sat in silence, Elle considered her friend. Over the past two days, his eyes had lost much of the sparkle that intrigued her so. He looked his age, perhaps older, for the first time since they had met. He was a man in pain, and she was uncertain how to assuage that hurt.

"I didn't mean to damper your spirits so," he said after too long a pause. "Isolation rarely heals the soul; you should get off Roan for an afternoon. Megan and Lainie are taking everyone to see a movie. It would do you a bit of good. I've got my daughter's faithful hound to keep me company."

"Caroline had mentioned that, but I think I'll stay put," she replied. "I'm so used to the quiet of the cottage. I could use an afternoon lost in my notes. I only have four or five weeks to finish up my primary research."

Leith stared into the cold fireplace, appearing to be lost in a distant thought. Outside the rain continued to pelt the window.

"I have an idea," he said at last with a curious smile. "This afternoon, I'm hoping to bring Lyle and Hendry together so we can discuss the future of Aldermire. Otherwise the house will be empty. You would have unfettered access to the entire estate."

"I've got plenty to keep me busy," she replied.

"True, my dear, but perhaps you could help me with a problem."

"For you, Leith, gladly."

"Let me give you a little history of Roan Island," he began. "Some of this you may know, but some of it may be new to you. Humor an old man his stories.

"In the 1700s, the Cape Fear River was part of the network of waterways that fed the Carolinas. Eagle Island was a bustling source of lumber, pitch and everything else that made shipping possible. And where there is shipping history, there is a darker history. Roan was an ideal last stop before Eagle Island for smugglers, pirates and every other lowlife wishing to avoid the eyes of the Colonial guard.

"Roan also provided one unique geographic feature not common to the lowland islands. It is the only island along the Cape Fear River with a solid foundation and enough elevation to support tunnels. The original house at Aldermire was connected to several outbuildings by a small but impressive network of carefully hidden tunnels. From the Aldermire basement one could travel to the dock, the northern seawall or the cottages completely undetected."

"The cottages?" Elle asked with a bit of concern.

He laughed in response. "Don't worry, my dear, they are tunnels no longer. As children, Hendry, I and the others would play along the dark corridors. It made for great mischief. Soon after Catheryn died, Hendry completed renovations of the main house and had them sealed. The tunnels themselves were filled to prevent collapse, and the entrances were walled off."

"How can I help you?"

"I tell you all of this for one reason," he said in his most conspiratorial tone. "Like the tunnels, there are countless other secrets buried at Aldermire, and secrets need to be explored and exposed."

"You've piqued my interest," she admitted.

"Hendry's wife Catheryn was a sharp woman. Few things escaped her eye. It has long been assumed that she knew more about Quacey's disappearance than she ever admitted. At the same time, she was fiercely loyal to her family. She would have done anything to protect her son and her clan.

"While she was alive, Catheryn kept those things most important to her in a carved rosewood lockbox. She kept it beneath her bed, and the key she wore around her neck in her mother's locket. When she died, the box went missing. I'd like you to see if you can find it."

"Do you think it is important?" Elle asked.

"I believe so," he replied, "not only to Quacey's death, but perhaps to Stuart's as well."

"What am I looking for?"

"It's a dark rosewood box, about the size of a football. It is beautifully carved with thistles and her name across the top. It should be unmistakable."

"Any suggestions on where to look?"

"Start in the attic," he suggested. "That should be a fairly quick search. The basement should be next, then the cottages. I'd have searched better myself, but age has been creeping up on me as of late. Those stairs will be the death of me, and heights have always terrified me. I'll keep Lyle and Hendry busy for a few hours. That should give you the run of Aldermire."

"Well, I could use the distraction," Elle agreed. "I'll give it today, then back to my research. Agreed?"

"Agreed. And one more thing, my dear," he leaned in with a serious expression. "Please, please be careful. I know the family is soldiering on, showing a stiff upper lip, pulling together in a time of adversity and all that rubbish. But never forget, we are very likely sharing a roof with Stuart's killer."

THOU SHALT NOT KILT

9

Oftentimes those tortured souls who fail to find fulfillment in life continue their search, caught between this world and the next. In the murky depths of the Cape Fear River off the coast of North Carolina, an American soldier lies forever separated from the woman he loved.

In 1810, Parian Lundie Duncan fell in love with Hannah Curstaidh MacUspaig, the legendary beauty of Aldermire Hall. A lowly farmhand, Parian was forbidden from courting the maid by Hannah's father. His daughter, he felt, should marry a man of means, one who could foster the economic prosperity Aldermire had long enjoyed.

The young couple carried on behind the elder Mac Uspaig's back, and she refused even the most ardent suitors—much to her father's consternation. At night, Parian would row his small boat to Roan Island and creep through dank tunnels to be with his lady love.

In October 1812, he used the familiar cover of darkness to traverse the Cape Fear River and visit Aldermire. He had news to share with Hannah: he was leaving to join the American forces in the great War of 1812. His luck, however, ran out as he landed on the is-

land's southern edge. Hannah's father and his men ambushed the couple and dragged Hannah, kicking and crying, from the man she loved. Parian was taken to the southern bulwark and shot through the head. His body tumbled into the river, never to surface.

Hannah never spoke to her father again, nor did she ever marry. Over the years she became known as the Gray Maid of Aldermire, a reclusive figure rarely seen by those outside the family. Upon her death in 1866, she was interred in the MacUspaig family crypt on Roan Island. Per her dying wish, an empty vault was sealed off beside her own, the ghostly resting place of her long-departed lover.

Over the years, both ghosts have been observed by several witnesses. Hannah, it is said, wanders the halls and tunnels of Aldermire dressed all in white. She forever searches for her true love. She never interacts with visitors, instead spending her afterlife moving from room to room hoping for any sign of Parian. He can often be seen scouting the southern coast of the island, hunting for a safe way up the bulwark or the entrance to the long-closed tunnel that leads him to his lady.

Forever in the afterlife the two will continue searching, aching to find one another but destined to spend eternity alone.

— Emery Vaughn,
Haunted Hollows: The Ghosts of the Carolinas

Elle sat at the counter in the kitchen and stared at the rain drumming in light, uneven ribbons against the large window overlooking the back lawn. Rows of alder trees and Lainie's carefully tended gardens drank in the raindrops, anticipating a drenching to come later in the afternoon.

Her impromptu lunch consisted of a Scotch egg and a rich oatcake with Lainie's homemade fig preserves. Although reheated in the toaster oven, the egg itself was nearly underdone, just like Elle's own grandmother would make. The sausage filling was well seasoned with a little peppered heat, and the crumb coating was flavored with a variety of dried herbs.

The oatcake was another delightful surprise. Over her almost forty years, Elle had found most cakes fell far short of those prepared by her Aunt Celia. There was always something missing: the oaty richness, the hint of sweet or the sublime texture. Although several hours old, this oatcake maintained a warm, crisp texture. Lainie, Elle conceded, was a master with the griddle.

Her fig preserves were an unusual complement. Elle was more accustomed to almond butter, a sharp cheese or strawberry jam atop her cakes. The figs accented the gentle sweetness of the cakes while adding a new flavor that was welcome, if unexpected.

The familiar treats surprised Elle with a wave of nostalgia for her mother, her sister and her family home. Aldermire was a grand house, one steeped in history and the countless stories that entailed. It lacked the warmth of home, Elle noted. To her it was simply a collection of overlarge rooms, a maze of chambers without a purpose or a heart.

She finished a second egg (and a third oatcake) and dropped her dishes in the sink. As she refilled Angus' water bowl, she thought about Leith's request. The mystery surrounding Quacey's disappearance was a welcome respite from the tragedy of just days ago. The thought that there may be some connection intrigued her.

The box Leith described should be easy to spot, she reasoned, and she resolved to spend the afternoon on the hunt. If she came up empty-handed, she'd return to her research.

As she passed through the library toward the great hall, Elle heard voices in quiet conversation near the front foyer. She slowed her pace as the voices began to rise. Lyle, she guessed, was in as sullen a mood as ever.

"I'd be happier if you just went," he whispered, loud enough for Elle to hear from the next room. "I can handle everything here. You'll be in the way."

"How can you say that?" It was Caroline's voice this time. "I know what it will take to keep this foundation afloat."

"Coira's grand plans are the least of our immediate problems. We've gone over this before, and the house is all that's important. Trust me, I've got this handled."

"I hope you're right," Caroline replied without conviction.

Caroline suddenly stopped, and Elle felt an awkward silence flow from the front room.

"Hello?" the younger woman called.

"One sec, just finished lunch." Elle tried to appear spontaneous and casual as she strolled into the great hall.

"Elle, there you are!" Caroline blurted. "I've been looking for you everywhere." She was dressed head to toe in yellow, from her hat to her slicker to her rain boots. To Elle, she looked ready to go to sea, not to a movie.

"We are heading to the dock for Wilmington. Everyone is going. Well, Everyone except Lyle and the fathers. Last chance! You simply must join us, I can't imagine you want to stay cooped up in here for another day."

As she spoke, Lainie and Megan descended the grand stairs together, both dressed for the wet weather.

"Caroline, it sounds wonderful, but as I said before, I am so behind in my work," she stated with an appropriate frown. "And Leith has me working on a special project."

"Oh, my. Sounds exciting," Megan likely lied as she joined the group.

"Nothing too thrilling, just a scavenger hunt for some of his old research notes."

"Any idea where he left them?" Lyle asked.

"Not really, but he thinks he may have accidentally packed them away in the attic or the basement. I'll start there."

"Sounds dreadful," Caroline replied. "Can't they wait until tomorrow?"

"It's all part of the job," Elle replied with a shrug.

"Then I suggest you take a flashlight," Lyle offered. "There are lights in the attic, but they don't go very far. The basement isn't much better. I've been down there maybe half a dozen times during my life, and it isn't a safe place in the dark."

"Thanks for the tip," Elle said. Seizing the opportunity, she bowed out of the conversation. "I think I saw one next to the refrigerator. Better go grab it now." She retreated to the kitchen, grabbed the torch and pocketed two more dry oatcakes.

"Well, enjoy yourself. We'll be back after dinner," Caroline called from the far room. "Hope you find what you're looking for!"

The attic was accessible only through a slim door on the second-floor landing of the back stairs. A rickety flight of steps meandered between the walls of the guestrooms, ending abruptly at a second door. Age and moisture caused the door to stick, but Elle gave it a good shove and almost fell into the cavernous space.

To Elle, it felt very much like a cathedral with a long, narrow nave and several distant transepts. The ceiling vaulted overhead, an unruly mix of beams, wires and centuries' worth of patching jobs. A row of single lights hovered overhead, and they blazed to life as she flicked the ancient toggle switch beside the upper door. A dormer window at each end of the central axis provided little additional light, although they both confirmed that the rain had not yet slacked.

To her surprise, Elle found the space to be tidier and better organized than her imagination had prepared her. The few boxes she could see were stacked and labeled with care. The area was free of clutter and debris, although the dust had coated everything in sight with a thick layer of gray.

With no plan in mind, she checked the collection nearest the door. Several clear tubs marked "Xmas Decorations" were topped with wreaths and wire Christmas trees wrapped in old sheets. The transparent plastic made for short work of the section. Elle could see no trace of a wooden box among the bundled tinsels, garlands, ornaments and stockings.

The next few sections were easy searches as well. A stack of card tables and folding chairs was followed by a few larger, broken pieces of furniture. As Elle opened each dresser drawer and armoire door with care, she came up empty-handed. A few barrister's bookshelves were filled with old volumes of every sort: children's books, European histories, biographies and more. The only common thread was the network of tunnels the silverfish had burrowed through most. The remaining stacks were no more interesting than these.

After less than twenty minutes, she had made her way to the far end of the attic. Visibility was poor outside of the circles of light directly under each bulb, but a box like the one Leith had described should have been an easy find. Instead, her search turned up a child's rusty pedal car, a few old *Playboy* magazines tucked behind a chimney stack, what appeared to be a box of old bagpipe chanters and the desiccated remains of a long-dead rat.

In the farthest alcove, Elle discovered a jumble of furniture covered in a tattered quilt. The tartan fabric, once a rich cross-hatch of reds and blues, had faded with time, dampness and ambient light from the dormer window.

She brushed away a stray cobweb and yanked on the corner of the quilt. Elle suppressed the urge to scream as a crowd of faces greeted her own. The urge nearly won when one face began to move.

She had taken three involuntary steps backwards before her senses settled. The faces, she realized, belonged to half a dozen MacUspaig ancestors, each rendered with care in fine oils. The familiar face drawn back in terror she recognized as her own reflection in a dusty mirror. She paused to calm her nerves and swear under her breath.

"Who the hell would stack these this way?" she said aloud. The paintings and mirror were tilted without care against a tall shelf and an ancient settee. To Elle they looked as though they were holding court, a circle of nobles surrounding her own dusty, flushed countenance. She counted six portraits that were visible and perhaps three more stacked behind.

She wondered what forgotten slight had exiled this particular group to the back reaches of the attic. Perhaps they each were family members who had fallen out of favor.

While not always an attractive bunch, the people in the portraits clearly belonged to the same clan of kin. They shared a certain classic Scottish essence: Roman noses, pale skin, high foreheads and, although not as common as folklore would suggest, hair in various shades of red.

Her eyes drifted from their faces to her own. It was clear how well her reflection meshed with the other portraits. Despite the remarkable genetic diversity of the Scottish people—a patchwork mix of Anglo-Saxon, Scandinavian, Germanic and even African and Asian—Elle found that she shared much with the past MacUspaigs.

And like these ancestors, she was a descendant of Scottish immigrants, although her own family had crossed the Atlantic several centuries after the first MacUspaigs. Still, she considered herself an American. Even her sister, born in Aberdeen but raised in North Carolina, sported a wicked southern twang and none of the lilting Scottish brogue of their mother.

What the three Cunningham women also shared with the MacUspaigs was a passion for their mutual Scottish heritage. Both families valued a closeness to the clan, the importance of tradition and a respect for the dead. One way to pay respect to those dead, she knew, was to embrace the life you had been given.

"Mama always says, 'You're a long time dead,'" she recited aloud. "'So get busy living.'" And for Stuart MacUspaig, long time dead had come far too soon.

Elle steeled her resolve and returned the MacUspaigs portraits to their exile beneath the threadbare quilt. She crossed the length of the attic, flipped the light switch and made her descent back to the living at Aldermire.

The landing was quiet; the only sounds Elle heard were the steady rain and the distant rumble of thunder. The back staircase led her to the cramped coat room off the servants' dining room and the recessed door tucked in the back of the closet.

With the help of the flashlight she located a set of switches. She tried each, then several together in various combinations. The lights—she assumed there were lights—failed to respond. She stared into the darkness, checked the light in her hand and tried to forget every horror movie she had ever seen.

A dozen uneventful steps later, she was safely at the bottom of the basement stairs. The flashlight cast a wide beam around a gaping space filled with dark, irregular shapes. Unlike the attic, the basement looked to have been long forgotten. Debris littered the ground, and stacks of forgotten furniture were piled at random around pillars supporting the floor above.

The wall closest to the stairs was fitted with a jigsaw puzzle of fuse boxes and circuit breakers for the electrical systems around the estate. The remainder was covered in rough pine shelves from floor to ceiling. Each shelf was filled with old canning jars, discarded glassware and ruined pantry supplies. In a few places, the moisture had rotted the wood through, spilling the contents on the packed brick floor below. Everywhere the smell of decay and neglect permeated the air.

Without moving from where she stood, Elle used the flashlight to explore the length of the room. It was maybe twenty-five feet wide and some sixty feet long. At the far end, it turned a corner, following the general floorplan of the great house.

"Where to start?" she asked herself aloud.

She considered the stack circling a nearby pylon. The odd tumble of boxes, table legs and what she thought might be bicycle parts was as good a place to begin as any. Once the spoked wheels were moved aside, Elle was able to access the boxes with surprising ease. For her efforts, she was rewarded with dozens of worthless newspapers, mildewed children's clothing and a collection of shortbread biscuit tins whose colorful artwork had long since rusted away.

The next two piles proved equally fruitless, and Elle began to doubt her resolve. The box, no matter how easy to identify, could be hidden away anywhere in the unexplored space that stretched before her.

She may not have cared deeply for Stuart, but she did care about what had happened to him. That care, she reminded herself, didn't change the reality of her situation. No matter how hard she tried to convince herself otherwise, her current search was taking her research further off track. Without her research and the possibilities it might afford her, she could stumble backwards. She had been there before—and for far too long. She had no wish to go back.

Still, I'm here, she thought. *I'll give Stuart today, then it's all about me. It has to be.*

She resolved to approach the search methodically. She would check the perimeter, then tackle the individual piles. She walked the length of the basement, her light darting from wall to wall for any obvious place to set or hide a wooden box.

As she made her way to the corner, she reflected on what little she did know about Stuart's death. She agreed with the others: whoever killed Stuart was likely living at Aldermire. Coira and the MacFarlanes were possible culprits, although she doubted it. They had too much to lose and too little to gain from anything that happened at Aldermire. She knew Stuart's death threw the trio's plans to the wind, but Elle couldn't see any of them resorting to violence.

She trusted her gut on Megan. First, the new Widow MacUspaig could be many things—abrasive, sarcastic, even bitter—but Elle didn't peg her as a killer. Second, depending on the nature of the prenuptial agreement, she may have stood to benefit very little from his death. And third, Megan was a mother, and from what Elle had seen, a very protective one. Killing Stuart would put her at risk and, in turn, put Cade at risk. She couldn't imagine Megan risking her son's wellbeing for a savory taste of revenge.

Leith and Hendry had spent the entire night holed up in the MacUspaig patriarch's bedroom discussing the fallout of Stuart's announcement. She admitted there was a possibility that one or the other had slipped out unnoticed, but she didn't think it likely.

Out the door, down the steps, through the library, a quick chat with Stuart, then a dagger in the back? She estimated that either man would have to be gone for fifteen to twenty minutes. His absence would have been hard to miss.

On paper Lyle and Caroline had the most to gain from Stuart's death, and neither had an alibi for the time of his murder.

Then there was Cade. For as little interaction as they had had, Elle felt he was a stable young man. Smart and easygoing, he didn't strike her as the kind of teen who'd kill in cold blood. Of course, he was also off island, not that his absence was an airtight alibi. Plus, Elle wasn't sure how far the young man would go to protect his mother.

To Elle, Lainie was a wild card. Like Cade, she claimed to be off island the entire evening. Elle had no reason to doubt her. Her sister's death presented another wrinkle. There was no proof that the two events were connected, but the coincidence couldn't be ignored.

As she turned the far corner of the basement, she saw only more of the same. Haphazard stacks of furniture and discarded goods cluttered the floor; dilapidated shelves slouched against the walls. The task was beginning to overwhelm Elle, a search through a haystack for a needle that might be nowhere to be found.

The beam from the flashlight swept the furthermost wall, and Elle caught herself. Something wasn't quite right. As the light returned to the left corner, she cocked her head for a better view of the section of shelves. They were at a very odd angle, coming toward her on one side and receding on the other as though in perspective.

She picked her way across the floor, her speed tempered by her tendency to misplace her feet. As she approached the far corner, it was clear that the shelf had swung away from the wall. In fact, it tilted out at a significant angle.

Closer inspection revealed a carefully constructed door, a thick slab comprised of layers of wood disguised to look like one of the ever-present shelves. With her free hand, Elle gave the closest edge a tug, and it swung open with surprising ease. For all its weight and bulk, it pivoted on a well-oiled hinge still hidden from view.

Beyond the door, Elle could make out a simple tunnel with stone block walls and a loose brick floor. The passage was remarkably free of dirt and clutter, and the air smelled musty but dry. The beam from the flashlight suggested the tunnel extended perhaps forty feet before curving out of sight to the left.

As she considered her options, Elle's eye noticed something hanging in midair, just out of her arm's reach. A quick sweep of the light revealed a thin metal chain suspended from the vaulted ceiling. At the other end, a bald light bulb sat nestled in a vintage porcelain socket. Out of habit, Elle reached in and gave the chain a tug. To her surprise, the tunnel was soon lit with a warm electric glow.

Her luck changing, Elle felt her spirits rise. She had no idea what she had found, but she had found *something*. And it was a start. Switching off the flashlight, she stepped into the tunnel. Despite the narrowness of the space, the high ceiling gave her a sense of openness. The light made the comfort more certain.

Twenty paces past the door, the glow of the bulb began to lose its warmth. She turned the flashlight on again and followed the gentle curve of the tunnel another twenty paces. Just past the turn, she was stopped by a rough wall of dirt and rubble supported by a tower of wooden planks and crates.

To Elle's untrained eye, it didn't look like a cave-in. It looked intentional.

As she turned to retrace her steps back to the basement, she heard a click that was faint but unmistakable. In the far distance of the tunnel, *something* had been moved into place. Her heart racing, she broke into a sprint. She caught her breath as she approached the light overhead. Just past the suspended bulb, the door had closed.

Correction, she thought, despite her panic. *The door has been closed. That massive thing didn't swing shut on its own.*

In three seconds she was at the door. She pushed with her shoulder, but the impressive slab of oak failed to budge. With the handle end of the flashlight she hammered against the wood, calling out to anyone who might hear.

Stepping back, she examined the door. Her heart sank. There was no handle, no latch on her side. Just a small hole at waist height through which she could see nothing.

The narrow space suddenly felt more constricted as Elle's fears took hold. She again slammed the flashlight into the immobile door until she worried it might break. She scoured the walls for some crack or crevice that might reveal a path to freedom. The entire length of the tunnel was uniform and featureless. The stone blocks were worn, perhaps centuries old.

At the far end, she searched the impromptu dirt wall, prying apart wooden boxes and loose planks to no avail. Each piece she moved only revealed more dirt or older wood. After half an hour, she gave up.

Several minutes later she sat on a rickety crate under the solitary bulb, thankful for its meager light. As she fought to control her breathing, she tried to find a center within. After a few seconds she attempted to make peace with her situation.

They'll know to look for me, she thought. *They'll find me. God, I hope they'll find me.*

As she leaned back against the tunnel wall, she looked up at the bulb overhead. In a moment of inspiration, she snapped her fingers.

Aloud she murmured, "*Murder under Montmartre!*"

10

Deep into that darkness peering, long I stood there, wondering, fearing, doubting, dreaming dreams no mortal ever dared to dream before.

— Edgar Allen Poe, *The Raven*

Elle ensconced herself in the overstuffed library chair nearest the fireplace. Angus warmed her feet while the fire took care of the rest. A small bowl of ice water helped numb the pain in her fingers but did little to assuage her pride.

"Wait, wait, wait," Cade exclaimed, shaking his head. "Run through that one more time. This is unreal!"

Elle held her head in her good hand. She tried not to make eye contact with any of the family members standing around the chair.

"I was trying to unscrew the light bulb," she said.

"What?" Megan cackled. "You're trapped in some godforsaken tunnel and you try and kill the best light you've got? Are you insane?"

"Maybe," Elle responded with a shrug. "It had been over an hour, and I was getting panicky. I had read about something like this in a book."

"Like what?" Cade asked.

"The heroine was trapped in a tunnel under the streets of Paris," Elle replied. "She was able to strip some of the wire from the wiring above her head and make the lights at Montmartre blink on and off." She paused.

"Keep going," Megan prodded.

"She relayed her position using Morse code. She got rescued and caught the German spy who was murdering the French scientists. It was actually a pretty good book, all things considered."

Megan lost herself in a fit of laughter. "Do you even know Morse code?"

Elle started to reply when she realized that Megan had a good point—a good point for which she had no answer.

"Turns out the bulb was really, really hot," she said instead.

"My dear, you're lucky you didn't electrocute yourself," Leith offered. "I shudder to think of what could have happened to you."

"What fool's errand were you on down there?" Hendry asked. She glanced at Leith, and he subtly shook his head. She paused for time.

"With the rain coming down, I was stuck here at the big house. I thought I'd search the place for anything relevant to my research. The basement seemed like a good idea at the time. Not so much now."

"Those damn tunnels are a danger," Hendry continued. "That's why I had them filled in years ago. You're a damn lucky girl."

"It was the rain that kept us home, too," Caroline said. "We were about to set off, and the wind started to whip up the waves. We came back to the house. When you didn't turn up, we went looking for you."

Megan shrugged. “I had no idea that tunnel even existed. Hell, I didn’t know we had a basement.”

“We were just starting to panic when you turned up,” Caroline added.

“How’d you get out?” Cade asked.

“The light bulb idea didn’t work so well, and all I got was singed fingers,” Elle replied. “Well, I got hungry, and I was deciding how to ration the oatcakes I had in my pocket. Right next to them I felt the ring of estate keys. Turns out the long skinny brass one was a perfect fit for the keyhole on the tunnel side of the door.”

“So you could have walked out at any time?” Megan asked.

“Yup, that’s about right. There was a small latch on the outside, but I just needed the key to open it from my side.”

“Lyle, get the damn thing sealed off,” Hendry barked. “The next fool might not be so lucky.”

“Maybe tomorrow,” Lyle replied as he headed for the front hall. “Right now I need to check the outbuildings. The storm coming off the Atlantic is going to be a bruiser. We might be in for a day or two of a deluge. Lainie, keep some dinner warm for me. I’ll be back in thirty minutes or so.”

“If you come up missing, we’ve already got the search party ready,” Megan offered with a wicked smile. “And since no one is willing to ask the question, I will. Who do you think locked you up in there, Elle? Or are we all agreeing to pretend it was the wind and head off to dinner.”

Elle shrugged. The room fell still, and the remaining family members regarded each other in silence.

“Speaking of dinner, I’ve had everything ready for a while,” Lainie said awkwardly. “Best to eat it before it goes cold. Just give me a minute to get the dishes out.”

"Leith and I will eat in my room," Hendry said, rising from his chair. "Still much to discuss."

After they left, Megan turned to her son. "Cade, honey, give Lainie a hand." A stern look suggested it wasn't up for negotiation. As he left for the kitchen, she closed the door behind him.

"Nice try," she said, focusing her attention on Elle. Caroline appeared to be doing her best to stay out of the line of fire.

"Come again?" Elle replied.

"You were poking around for 'research' in some crumbling tunnel buried under Aldermire? I don't believe you."

Again, Elle considered a sharp retort but thought better of it.

"You could have gotten hurt down there," Caroline added with overstated concern.

"Listen, it's a long story."

"Dinner can wait. I've got no place to be," Megan replied, taking the seat directly across from Elle. "Spill it."

Elle opted for honesty. Without stating names, she recalled her conversation with Leith, describing the box and its potential relevance to both suspicious deaths.

"You're saying it might connect Stuart's murder to this Quacey's disappearance?" Megan asked with clear disbelief. "We were only married for a few years, but it was something he just wouldn't talk about. I knew he had been married before, but living with him you'd never know it."

"Whatever is in the box might give us all some hint as to why they were killed," Elle replied. "It may be nothing, but it could also be an important clue to what happened."

"A clue? So now you're Miss MacMarple? This is too good."

"Laugh if you want, but like I told you before, I owe Stuart at least this."

Megan nodded and shrugged. "I can respect that."

"I don't want to intrude," Caroline interjected. Her voice made the other two women jump. She had been uncharacteristically quiet, and Elle had forgotten she was in the room.

"And I don't want to spread rumors," she continued, "but when I was a little girl, I used to hear stories about parts of the MacUspaig family fortune hidden around the island. Supposedly all trace of the treasures disappeared about the same time as Hendry's wife died. If she kept her best secrets in this box, do you think there might be a connection?"

Megan and Elle looked at each other. Elle shrugged.

"I've never heard of a MacUspaig fortune," Megan replied, "but given everything Stuart didn't tell me, it could be a thing."

Caroline's natural chattiness quickly returned.

"I hadn't thought about it in years, but perhaps it's all connected," she continued, staring into the fireplace. "I know it might be a huge coincidence, but it would certainly make sense. If you're going to hide treasure, Roan Island would be a perfect spot. I just can't imagine what the fortune may be. With all the smuggling and sneaking around at Aldermire, it could be *anything*. Maybe pirate's gold or Colonial silver or who knows what.

"And if there is a treasure, I can only wonder who would own it today. There have to be, like, time limits, or whatever they call those. Oh, *statutes of limitations*, that's the phrase I was thinking of. Would the MacUspaigs still own the treasure? If it turns out that Lyle owns Aldermire, could we sell it to museums or collectors? What do you all think it could be?"

Without a word, the other two women rose and exited to the dining room, leaving Caroline to answer her own questions.

Dinner was a quiet affair. The close quarters were beginning to wear on Elle, and she suspected the others were feeling the strain. The conversation was sparse, and the mood remained tense.

Even Caroline was quieter than usual, Elle observed, although she wasn't sure whether to attribute it to the dour company or the visions of buried treasure dancing through the younger woman's head.

A few minutes after the meal began, Leith entered the dining room and took a seat between Elle and his daughter. Hendry's mood, he noted, was continuing to deteriorate.

"I had hoped the company here would be inviting," he whispered to Elle as the others ate the meal in silence. "Perhaps not."

Lainie had spent the afternoon in the kitchen on dishes that could be easily reheated over the coming days. A few frozen chicken breasts coupled with vegetables from the garden yielded a warm, spicy cock-a-leekie soup. A touch of whiskey made the savory broth a welcome end to a wet, windy day. Two bowls of fried skirlie and piping hot clapshot provided filling side dishes that would carry them through the long night ahead.

"My dear, you are a culinary wizard." He beamed. "Next you'll be turning water into wine."

Lainie looked up from her plate with a slight smile. "I haven't been to Saint Andrews in a few days, and we're starting to run low in the kitchen. Until the storm passes, we'll be making due with what we have left."

"With you in charge, we'll eat like kings," her father said, raising his glass to his daughter. "You know, isolation isn't uncommon here on Roan Island. When the island served as a stop for ships traveling the Cape Fear River, the family and its servants could go months or more without visiting the mainland. Between food grown at Roan, stored provisions, and supplies delivered by passing boats, the MacUspaigs could last months without a trip to Wilmington or Saint Andrews."

"Sounds like they had everything they needed in one place," Lyle responded as he downed a full tumbler of whiskey. Elle was surprised he was paying attention. Throughout dinner he had looked distracted, almost vacant.

"Very true, Lyle," Leith replied. He scratched his chin for a moment. "Roan can be an island, quite literally, unto itself. Spend too long here and one can forget the world outside. It is a seclusion that comforts but also isolates."

Lainie returned her eyes to her dinner. "I haven't left the island in two days, and already it feels like a lifetime." Her gaze shifted from the plate in front of her to the windows overlooking the lawn. "I know every inch of this island, maybe too well. There's an entire world out there beyond the river just going to waste."

Lyle followed her gaze to the window. "Who needs the world?" he asked. "I've got everything I need right here. I guess it's just a matter of perspective. I've lived here my entire life under Stuart's thumb. Now it looks like Roan and Aldermire are going to end up in my hands. I don't mind saying that this old house is much more comfortable now that I know it's mine." He lifted his own glass in a toast to no one. "The rest of the world can go to hell."

After dinner, Elle returned to her room. Angus took roost on a small oriental rug by her nightstand, something that surprised Elle and seemed welcome by Lainie. As she sat on the edge of the bed, she pulled a silk-cased pillow to her lap. The cool of the fabric calmed her nerves like a refreshing breeze. Two deep breaths and she felt a temporary peace.

The sudden tears surprised her, and they came in rivers. Her strength was her pride. She had been through so much and still, she survived. She survived on her own terms and in the manner in which she chose.

She hadn't shown it—or even realized it—that evening, but the situation in the tunnel had affected her to the core. The fear, the isolation and the helplessness lasted less than an hour. Yet still they tore at who she believed herself to be and who she needed to be.

Sequestered on Roan Island, Elle wanted to hear that she'd be alright. She wanted to hear a voice of comfort and care. She wanted to talk to Lana. Elle's sister was the one person who had never lost faith in her. No matter how poor Elle's choices had been, Alana had been there.

She closed her eyes and took three slow breaths. Elle knew that facing the coming days alone would be a challenge. She had exhausted her reserves following Stuart's death, and now she was running on empty.

"I need to do this on my own," she whispered aloud.

After three more deep breaths, she found her center. Four minutes later she was ready to turn in. Pulling the covers to her chest, she reached down to scratch a slumbering Angus behind the ears and clicked off the nightstand lamp. She lay on the bed and watched the shadows of the trees outside ripple across the bedroom. The ambient voices of Aldermire pricked her ears. She counted to five, clicked the light back on, stepped over her lackadaisical watchdog and locked her door for the first time since coming to the great house.

Back in bed, she again doused the light. She focused on the snoring dog and the sound of endless rain against the tall windows. It lent a steady, deep rhythm to her breathing. Despite her fears that it would never come, she soon drifted into a restful, dream-filled sleep.

In her dream she once again walked the twisting halls of Aldermire. In her deepest subconscious, she was aware that something was different. Although her sleeping self couldn't place it, the MacUspaig portraits were missing. The watchful eyes that judged her movements were gone. In their place stood two rows of figures covered in tattered sheets, one row along each wall.

From where she stood in the center of the hall, she couldn't tell if the figures were marble or human, perhaps just bodies. Her instincts told her it was a question best left unanswered.

Between each pair of statues was a door. As she walked down the hall, she passed between two doors, then two figures, then doors, then figures until she lost track of how far she had wandered.

Her curiosity piqued, she tried a door and found it locked. Its twin across the hall was locked, too. Three more doors convinced her that they provided no exit from the hallway she traveled.

At one, she placed her ear against the wood. To her surprise, she heard a pair of voices. She couldn't discern their genders, their ages or even the language they spoke. She cupped her hand against the door and still the voices remained a mystery. The door across the hall muffled the same pair partaking in an identical conversation. Every door she listened at provided more of the same.

As Elle listened closer, she began to decipher the mood. The voices sounded complicit, almost conspiratorial, in their tone. Whispers and innuendo were peppered with the quiet laughter of a shared joke. Over time the conversation took a more heated timbre. The clandestine disposition of the voices blossomed into something more suggestive, perhaps even carnal. Although she couldn't make out a single word, Elle felt her chest and neck flush red in embarrassment.

She pulled back from the door and stepped down the hall, fanning away the heat rising from her own discomfort. As the muffled voices reached a crescendo, her walk broke into a run until the covered figures to either side were flying past her in a blur of shapeless white.

Elle woke to a clap of thunder just beyond the safety of Aldermire's stone walls. She found herself on top of the sheets, sweating despite the chill in the air. Her heart was racing as her senses fought to focus.

She slipped on a robe, unlatched her bedroom door and looked out into the hall. The house was too still. No lights illuminated the landing, and the only sound was the muffled, distant murmur of the wind and rain. She listened for another minute. Her nervousness fading, she made her way to the small sitting area above the back stairs.

Elle repositioned an overstuffed chair until she could sit with her back square against the wall. She lifted the landline's receiver and dialed. Her sister picked up on the second ring.

"Are you okay?" Lana asked, not bothering with a hello. The voice was a warm hug in the cool emptiness of Aldermire.

"You sound awake," Elle replied with relief.

"My baby sister calls me at 3 a.m. Trust me, I'm awake. Just tell me you're alright. Promise me Stuart's killer doesn't have you at knifepoint or anything."

"I promise."

"Not that you could say so anyway if he had a knife to your throat," Lana replied. "You swear?"

"All the time." Elle smirked. "And yes, I swear on Mama's grave."

"Mama's grave? Baby girl, that's just wishful thinking," Lana replied with a muffled laugh. "Hold on, Ellie, Sophie's got an early morning. Gonna slip into my office."

Over the connection, Elle heard a door close gently. The relief of hearing Lana's voice brought her a sudden, profound sense of calm.

"So are you really okay?"

"Big picture, I'm fine," Elle said. "Just a bad dream, and I needed to hear your voice."

"Ellie, you aren't the bad dream type," Lana said with concern. "How many times have you called me after midnight in the past thirty years?"

"Well, not counting bail calls or 'I need a lift home from wherever the hell I am' calls, none that I can remember." Lana laughed again.

"What's got you spooked?"

"It's a lot of things," Elle replied. "It's Stuart's death. It's being cooped up on the island. It's this family. It's just everything." She decided to gloss over her misadventures from the previous afternoon.

Lana let the words hang for a moment. "Elle, there's something going on in your head. I'm not gonna push, but I know you."

"I think Stuart's death has kicked the wind out of me. It was a shock, but that's wearing off. Sitting here in this house, the shock is turning into fear. Lana, I think I'm scared."

"Baby girl, if you're scared, I'm scared. You need to pack your bag and get the hell out. Simple as that."

Elle took a deep breath. "It's not that easy, Lana. I've been working so hard these past few months to keep it all together. No matter how bad it's gotten, I've never been one to run away from something. I don't know, it would just feel like defeat. I almost didn't call you. I didn't want you to think I couldn't handle this."

Elle heard her sister take a deep breath. "Ellie, you are the strongest, fiercest, bravest woman I know."

"Lana, I'm not brave. You've always been the brave one."

"Sorry, little sister, but you're the brave one. I'm the stable one," she replied. "And trust me, it's easy being stable. For me, being brave means mixing my whites and lights on laundry day. For me, that's a rush." It was Elle's turn to laugh.

"Which one of us was brave enough to say, 'Screw it' and walk empty-handed out of a lousy marriage? Which one of us could turn homelessness and hopelessness into one hell of a research opportunity? Hell, I've seen you stare down Mama over the last piece of Aunt Celia's sweet potato pie and win. You're a damn warrior, girl."

"In all fairness, her pie is totally worth dying for," Elle replied.

"Baby girl, let me give you two pieces of sisterly advice. First, don't sell yourself short. You are more amazing than you know. I look at what you've been through and what I know you're still going to accomplish, and I envy you that strength. Second, trust your instincts. Get the hell out. Now. In fact, I can meet you at Moira's Café this morning. Heck, I'll swim over myself right now and carry you back before the sun comes up."

"I don't deserve you, Lana," Elle said with an audible sigh of relief.

"Ellie, you deserve so much more. Let's just get you out of there. I talked to Sophie the day before yesterday, and she's happy to put you up in the guest room for a while. And the boys are just nuts about their amazing Auntie Elle."

"Sophie said that?" Elle asked with skepticism.

"Okay, one more piece of advice," Lana replied. "You need to get over this thing you think Sophie has about you. Believe it or not, she adores you."

"She just always seems short with me. Never sure why."

"I can tell you why. She thinks the world of you, but most days she wants to smack you upside your head. She knows you're too smart for some of the choices you were making."

"And now I'm just flitting around with no plan and no real job."

"Let me give it to you straight. Sophie thinks that you are living in a castle on an island, writing best sellers and crawling through tombs like Indiana Jones. Meanwhile, she's got a dental practice, a wife, two kids, two woefully inadequate college funds and a mortgage. To her, you're living a life right out of the movies."

Elle laughed again. "Lana, you have no idea how badly I needed this," she said.

"Any time, Ellie. So you are coming back to Saint Andrews in the morning?"

"Give me a day. I have stacks of notes to box up, and the grant committee won't wait forever. If I can get everything packaged up tomorrow, I'll have Miller's ferry pick me up the next morning. And tell Sophie I'll only be there a few days. Tell her I have an ark to raid."

"It's a deal. Stay safe until then. I miss you, baby girl."

The clock read 4:12 a.m. as Elle stepped over Angus and crawled back into bed. Lana had calmed her nerves, but her earlier dream still knocked around in her head. The voices heard through the door sparked some memory, some nearly forgotten scene that Elle felt she should recall.

As the clock turned to 5:00 a.m., the pieces began to fall into place. The voices on the other side of the hallway door were the voices she was now certain she heard coming from the white cabin on the night of Stuart's murder. She still didn't recognize the pair, but the conspiratorial, carnal nature of their conversation was now a distinct memory.

"Who?" was the question she struggled with. She could discount Stuart, as he was with her, however briefly. Leith and Hendry were in the MacUspaig patriarch's bedroom. Megan was an unlikely choice, and Cade and Lainie were off island. That left Lyle and Caroline.

Still, it struck Elle as odd behavior for a married couple. Why lie about their rendezvous if it means leaving each other without an alibi for Stuart's murder?

Her tired mind wandered for a few minutes before returning to Cade and Lainie. Ostensibly, they had been in town seeing a movie. Perhaps they had returned earlier than they claimed. Had they docked just after the ferry left with Coira and the others, they would have had ample time to meet up at the white cottage before returning to Aldermire.

Lainie is nearly fifteen years older than Cade, she thought, *but it wouldn't be unheard of.* And Elle could understand their decision to meet away from Aldermire. Hooking up under the same roof as Megan could have led to disaster. "She'd kill them," she whispered aloud. Elle immediately regretted her choice of words.

The longer she lingered on the idea, the more sense it made. There simply wasn't any other reasonable explanation. *The last question is a bit trickier,* she thought. *What do they have to hide?*

11

The funeral held at noon was all completed, and the last stragglers of the mourners had taken themselves lazily away, when, looking carefully from behind a clump of alder trees, we saw the sexton lock the gate after him.

— Bram Stoker, *Dracula*

As the sun crested over the east end of Roan Island, Elle lay awake in bed. Sleep had never returned, but, to her surprise, she felt rested and focused. She had a full day to collect her research and retreat to Saint Andrews.

She showered and changed into jeans and a faded t-shirt. She pinned her curls back into a messy bun, considering it a job well done. Any thoughts of keeping up appearances when mingling among the MacUspaigs had ended with Stuart's death.

There was no sign of life in Aldermire's kitchen. Angus returned to his favorite spot next to the back door, and food in his bowl suggested that Lainie was up and around at an early hour. Despite that conclusion, Elle found no breakfast waiting for her.

She shrugged, checked the refrigerator for any leftover oatcakes, found none and resigned herself to bran flakes with fresh fruit. The sound of cereal hitting the bowl brought the hound to her feet. He sat dutifully watching her eat, clearly hoping she was as clumsy as she looked. Elle was hungry, eating every bite with uncharacteristic care.

"Sorry, little guy," she said, "I don't mess around with food." He licked her ankle and followed around the kitchen as she washed her bowl and set it in the drainer. As a reward for his attention, she gifted him with two baby carrots from the crisper drawer. Angus double-checked the floor under her chair before collapsing on his bed near the door.

As she considered making a trip to the red cottage for the first box of her notes, Elle heard the phone ring in a distant part of the house. Doors opened and closed, and the ringing stopped. A few moments later, she heard footfalls on the back stairs, and Leith entered the kitchen with a warm welcome.

"My dear, you're up early!" he exclaimed. "I was worried that the phone might have woken you, given the trying events of yesterday. I must say you are looking a bit more like your old self. I was worried about you."

"I'm feeling more like my old self, too," she admitted. "Yesterday threw me a curve ball, but my nature is to swing for the fences."

"Speaking of the phone, that was our dear Detective Tanner. He will be over shortly," he said and rolled his eyes. "As soon as he finds a ride. It appears the department has only one boat available for his use, and it is being serviced. He would like to speak to us all. Perhaps a few questions, as well. He wasn't very specific. With the tempest coming in off the Atlantic, he may not have another chance with us for a few days."

"Are you and Lainie staying on Roan through the storm?" she asked. "It looks like it will be worse than what we've already had."

"My dear, Aldermire has weathered worse and still she stands. Storm or no storm, I hope to live out the rest of my days here on Roan. For nearly thirty years now I've had the good fortune to call this remarkable place my home. I've made countless friends here, raised two daughters here and, God willing, I'll die here."

He paused for a moment.

"Elle, just a few days ago I told you that losing a child was a parent's greatest fear. I may have misspoken. The more I am aware of my own mortality, the more I worry about the child I'll leave behind. Lainie is a remarkable girl, and Aldermire is the only home she's truly known. We both moved here shortly after Quacey's wedding at Hendry's insistence, and, except for a few days here and there, she's never spent much time anywhere else.

"In my old age, I worry that Roan hasn't been the best home for her," he continued. "The isolation I spoke of last night can be very damning. With too much time spent cut off from humanity, the soul can turn in on itself. Basic goodwill becomes corrupted, the senses shed their perspective and the world loses its magic. It's a miserable way to live, and one I've witnessed firsthand. My dear, I pray every day that my foolish choices haven't damned her to such a life."

He crossed the kitchen to the sink and retrieved a clean mug. He poured his morning coffee with care. "This, I believe, is the true burden of being a parent. We are tasked with tending to every need for those special souls we love most, until the day we must trust them to weather the world once we are gone."

"You are a remarkable man and an exemplary father," Elle assured him. "Lainie can't help but know how much she is loved. My father died before I was born. I only know him through the pictures and the stories my mother squirrels away in her scrapbooks. Had God given me the choice, I'd have wished for a dad like you."

Leith gave a small laugh and rolled his eyes. "My dear, how little you know me," he said. "I am an imperfect man perfectly suited for an imperfect world."

"But you care and you try. That's more than most children can hope for," she said, giving him a hug around his shoulders. "Speaking of isolation, I have to tell you something. I plan on leaving Aldermire tomorrow." Her words elicited an immediate response.

"Elle, please tell me you aren't abandoning your work here," he exclaimed. "Your research is so unique, so important. The stories you're documenting may never be told again, once the likes of Hendry and me are gone."

"Leith, I'm still committed to the research and the grant," she replied. "To be honest, I need the grant funding to live on for the next two or three months. With Stuart's death, Aldermire has changed. I've always preferred my tragedies after the fact. This one hit far too close to home, and it's shaken me."

He shook his head slowly. "I hate to agree with you, but I understand," he said at last. "Just promise me you'll tell the stories of clans like the Dalerochs and the MacUspaigs."

"I will," she replied.

"If you need any help collecting your work, please let me know. I will always support your gifted research into such a fascinating field. And before I forget, I'll get you a copy of notes on the silver buttons we found. It may not be much, but it may tie together a few loose threads."

"With any luck, I will be back in a week or two," she said. "I need to clear all of this with Megan or Lyle or whomever the hell owns this place now, but I'm not expecting any resistance. I can complete my first-person work then with two weeks left for the initial draft. It's not ideal, but I think I'll be more focused than I am here."

"Again, I understand," he replied. From above the kitchen, the pair heard the first footfalls. "I should go and let the rest know to expect young Detective Tanner."

He returned her hug and retreated to the back stairs.

For thirty minutes Elle watched Jeannie Pace attempt to engage the family in small talk concerning the house, the gardens and the weather. Every volley landed on the library floor without notice. Even the dog seemed uninterested in the deputy's attention.

While Detective Tanner spoke with Hendry and Leith in the dining room, Elle regarded the remaining members of the Aldermire estate. Lyle and Caroline sat on opposite ends of the tapestry-covered couch. They had no words for one another, and each looked lost in thought. Lainie was dressed for outdoor work, her jeans and hands dusted with soil from the gardens. Cade napped, or pretended to, in a large library chair while his mother thumbed through an old coverless *National Geographic* magazine.

Elle bided her time with Angus at her side. He pressed his body against her chair as she scratched under his impressive ear. Every few seconds she'd stop, and he would nudge her fingers in supplication for more.

After another twenty minutes, Jonah Tanner opened the dining room door and ushered the patriarchs back into the library. As the two old men took their chairs, Deputy Lewis took his place by the French door. With a raised hand, Jonah asked for the family's attention.

"First of all, I want to thank you for your patience," he said. "I know these past two days have been very difficult for you all. Please trust that we are doing everything we can to find out exactly what happened to Mr. MacUspaig. Our team has gathered a good deal of physical evidence, and we're working around the clock to sort this out."

Caroline looked around the room and raised her hand. "Officer Tanner?"

"*Detective* Tanner. Yes, Mrs. MacUspaig?"

"Does this mean we're free to leave Roan Island?" she asked. "I don't want to be disrespectful, but I think we're all starting to get a little stir crazy." She looked around the room again, appearing to search for nods of support. She came up empty-handed. "Regardless," she continued, "Lyle and I would like to stay a few days in Saint Andrews, just to get away from this house for a bit."

Jonah shrugged. "Feel free to come and go as you need, but I ask you to stay close. We may need to speak to any of you with fairly short notice, in case we have any additional questions."

"My good boy, when do you plan on leaving?" Leith asked Lyle.

"Sooner rather than later. And just for a few days. I'd be happy staying, but Carrie has it in her head that we need a break from Aldermire."

"Actually, if you could meet me in Saint Andrews, that would be a huge help," Deputy Pace interjected. "It's not an easy thing, but there's some paperwork we'll need you to sign.

Most regards how and to whom we should release Mr. Mac Uspaig's body. It will make final arrangements much easier."

At the mention of a funeral, the room fell silent.

"With all the confusion, I hadn't even thought about how we would handle that," Lyle admitted. "Wouldn't that be something for Megan to take care of?"

Megan raised her hands. "I'll pass. Let's just say my heart isn't in it."

"Fine, I'll figure something out," Lyle replied. "We can have Stuart released to Montrese & Sons in Wilmington. He can be interred in the family crypt."

Hendry gave a harsh laugh and stood from his chair by the fireplace. "Like hell he will," he said. "Stuart spat on his family name and cast our legacy aside. He'll enter that sacred place only long after my time on Earth is over."

His bile appeared to catch the family members off guard, and the room again fell silent.

"There will need to be some sort of gathering to memorialize his life," Leith suggested. "Wherever he may be put to rest. We should revisit this tomorrow. Perhaps we'll have a different perspective then."

Jonah looked from Leith to Hendry to Lyle. "Mr. Mac Uspaig, um, Lyle, please just let me know where to reach you in Saint Andrews. We can take care of the formalities at the station. I'll leave you and the family to figure what happens then. Any other questions?"

He looked around the room and, receiving no response, thanked them for their time. As the family began to drift from the room, he caught Elle's eye and gave a quick nod.

"Any chance I could speak to you and Mrs. MacUspaig for a moment?" he asked. "In private would be best."

Deputies Lewis and Pace walked ahead as Jonah held back with the two women.

"So, detective, just wanted to arrest us in private? Not make a big scene? Risk a real MacUspaig throwdown?" Megan asked as they stopped just beyond the house.

"No such luck," Jonah responded. "Although the idea is starting to sound better and better."

Megan rolled her eyes. "At this point, if it gets me away from this damn family, consider me guilty."

"Should I consider that a confession?" he asked.

"Let's just call it a plea for mercy," she replied.

"What do you need to talk to us about?" Elle interjected to move the conversation along. *I'd rather be back at the red cottage packing up my papers,* she thought.

"First, is there anything you can tell me that the others may have failed to mention?" he began. "Anything at all."

Elle and Megan regarded each other for a moment, and Elle shook her head.

"I'm guessing Leith detailed my little adventure in the basement," Elle said at last.

"He did," Jonah replied. "While I talked to them, Lewis took a look around down there. Came up empty-handed. Any idea who'd want to keep you locked up in that death trap?" He glanced at Megan.

"I can't say it hasn't crossed my mind," Megan admitted with a laugh. "I still had no idea we even had death traps on Aldermire. And right under my very feet. It would have made life so much easier."

"Seriously, Elle, any idea who? Or why?" he repeated.

"None at all," Elle replied. "After I told Leith I'd be looking around down there, I also told Lyle and Caroline. And she loves to talk. Oh, and Megan and Lainie were there as well. I have no idea who else knew."

"To be honest, Caroline brought up it twice more by the time we reached the dock," Megan added.

Jonah took a few notes in his notebook. "Anything else you both think I should know?"

"Nothing comes to mind," Elle replied for them both. "If anything does, we'll give you a call right away."

Megan gave the detective a sly glance. "Is there anything at all *you* can tell us about Stuart?"

Jonah closed his notebook and surveyed the two women. "I didn't want to say this in front of the family, but there were no prints on the weapon. And everyone on the island had easy access to the knife. So that doesn't narrow it down. Unless we missed something, the rain scrubbed all our physical evidence. We are stuck at zero."

"You're saying that, as far as the police know, any one of us could have killed my husband?" Megan asked.

"At this point, your guess is as good as mine," he replied with a sigh. "We did get back the toxicology report. Nothing surprising there. He had a few drinks in him, but his BAL didn't indicate impairment. He was loose but not drunk, not by a mile."

"Well, I can certainly vouch for that," Elle offered.

"Oh, and he had taken several doses of Priaptix." He paused, searching for the right words. "It's, well, a performance enhancer."

"An erectile dysfunction med?" Megan asked without skipping a beat.

Jonah nodded. "That would be it."

"I can vouch for that one, too," Elle noted, staring at the sky.

"What a right bastard," Megan muttered under her breath. "Please just tell me that's what actually killed him."

"It didn't kill him," Jonah said with a wary smirk, "but it made his last few moments harder than they needed to be." He smiled, clearly proud of the joke. Elle laughed, then felt immediate regret.

"How long have you had that one locked and loaded?" she asked.

"Since I got the report this morning," he replied. To Megan he added, "Sorry about that, ma'am. It was inappropriate and not very professional."

"I'm not losing any sleep over it," she replied. "What's the saying? 'He died as he lived,' I think. In any case, it is just so fitting."

He put the notebook in his breast pocket and ran his fingers through his short hair.

"One thing I forgot to mention back there is that I'll be talking to each of you again over the next few days," Jonah concluded. "It's always useful to see who switches their story as their memory changes. With the physical evidence we have, or more accurately don't have, my best chance to figure this out is hoping someone trips themselves up. And Elle, keep your eyes open and stay away from all death traps," he suggested. "Okay?"

"Will do."

Elle and Megan walked back to Aldermire in silence. As they approached the grand terrace, Elle begged off and turned toward the pair of guest cottages. She looked to the eastern end of Roan and picked up her pace. A heavy sky was darkening over the Atlantic, portending an evening, perhaps more, of torrential rain.

Growing up in the Carolinas, Elle had lived through her share of ocean-born storms. The winds whipped the waves to towering peaks while the billowing clouds dimmed the midday sun to a hazy, red-tinged twilight.

Two days after her eighth birthday, Saint Andrews had been pummeled by a deluge that sprang up in an instant, just beyond the south end of the Cape Fear River. Despite Elle's protests, her mother had collected her daughters and huddled over them in the first-floor bathroom of their small wooden-framed home. Near hurricane-strength winds shook the walls and tested the windows as Gavina recited traditional prayers in an old Scottish dialect Elle barely understood.

When the storm passed, Elle stood on the home's rickety front porch and witnessed firsthand the awesome power of nature. Most houses along their street had sustained damage, two having lost parts of their roofs. Glass, shingles and unidentifiable debris littered their narrow street. It was several more years before her mother explained that their neighbor, Mrs. Chautis, hadn't moved to California, but instead had been killed, struck by an airborne sheet of wooden siding.

She had never again questioned the wisdom of deferring to the side of safety. Despite the obvious danger Stuart's death laid bare, Elle could think of fewer safer places to be than Aldermire's sturdy stone walls.

She reached the red cottage just as the wind on Roan began to stir the trees. The storm was still an hour or two off, but Elle had no wish to push her luck. The room was exactly as she had left it.

"One hell of a mess," she murmured. Two plastic tubs from the closet were soon filled with notebooks, photographs, photocopies and graphite rubbings.

Despite the jumble of names, dates and facts before her, Elle felt sure of one thing regarding the tragic history of Clan MacUspaig: it was still being written. She was accustomed to witnessing the rise and fall of a great family from a safe distance and a delay of several decades or even centuries. This was new ground for a researcher like Elle. She was living this story, actively participating in its narrative.

"But how will it end?" she asked herself as she closed the red cottage door and locked it tight ahead of the coming storm.

The tubs were light but awkward. The wind did little to ease her work as occasional gusts pulled her burden first left, then right. With only two short pauses to rebalance her load, Elle was soon standing in Aldermire's kitchen. She tucked the tubs behind the mudroom rack for easy access in the morning.

At the kitchen sink, she washed a series of graphite smudges off her fingers. Looking out the sink window, she saw Lainie, still dressed for outdoor work, tending several of the plants in the rear garden. Her motions looked rushed and harried, as though she were racing the storm.

Despite her desire to hide in her room until morning, Elle dried her hands and made her way out the servants' door and down to where Lainie stooped, collecting Shetland kale and cauliflower.

Elle flipped an empty basket over and sat on her makeshift chair before a trellised blackberry bush (*bramble* bush, her mother would say). Lainie immediately accepted the offer for help and gave Elle a quick tutorial on which berries were ready for quick picking. Within minutes the pair had a generous bucket nearly filled with the knobby, tart fruits.

"I know I won't get to everything," Lainie said as she continued harvesting handfuls of leafy kale, "but I want to pull a little of anything ripe so I have some variety over the next day or two."

"In the weeks I've been here, this is as close as I've gotten to the vegetable garden," Elle admitted.

"Did you grow up with a garden?"

"Mama was always growing something. Usually herbs, maybe tomatoes or squash. Never anything as amazing as this," she replied. She surveyed the manicured rectangles of vegetables, fruits and other plants she didn't recognize. "Who started all of this?"

Lainie shrugged. "Roan has always had vegetable gardens, and Father says that there have been rose gardens and other florals from time to time. The big formal gardens have been here longer than I have.

"I think these gardens were the idea of Mrs. MacUspaig, Hendry's wife. She was from an old Carolina family, and she had an amazing knowledge of plants, herbistry and old-fashioned mountaineering. When I was younger, she'd let me help her prune the vines at the end of the season, but my favorite was picking the berries." She smiled at the memory. "For a while we had both blackberries and raspberries. I probably ate more off the plants than I ever put in the baskets. But she didn't care. I think she just liked the company."

"What's in that area over there?" Elle asked, pointing to an odd hodgepodge of trees, bushes and other plants.

"That was old Hendry's idea," Lainie explained. "Like the alder trees that give Aldermire its name, all those plants come from Scotland. Every few years, he'd have different specimens sent over from the Highlands. The climate here can be a problem, but most Scottish plants are a hardy stock."

"Just like its people."

Lainie nodded. "True, but the plants are much easier to deal with."

"What does he have growing over there?" Elle pressed.

"Well, the alder trees all over Roan have been here as long as the house. He's had a few more brought over when the mood strikes. My favorite is the melancholy thistle. Those are the tall stalks over past the tomato cages. It loves lousy soil but still needs the dampness. The heather and furze add some color along the borders, and both love the coastal soil here on Roan. The second two rows are bog myrtle and nightshade. In front of that is a mix of foxglove, Scottish primrose and blue-sow thistle. I have no idea how we've gotten those last two to hang on here. They are nearly impossible to grow outside of Scotland."

"Aren't some of those dangerous?" Elle asked.

"Why do you think I keep them away from the vegetables?" Lainie replied. "Most of those we used to keep around for the original Mrs. MacUspaig's home remedies."

"Remedies?"

"She grew up with mountain medicine, and old Hendry was a great believer in home remedies. He still is, but his doctor would have a fit if he even suggested bog myrtle tea."

"What are they good for?" Elle asked.

"Well, bog myrtle was supposedly good for ulcers and fevers, especially if you make a tea from the leaves. Nightshade plasters were used for pain relief. Heather is a natural antiseptic. And foxglove is a very powerful diuretic. Of course, we've never used them since her death. But now they've just become a permanent part of the garden."

"So how long have you lived at Aldermire?" Elle prodded.

Lainie took a deep breath and looked off to the storm clouds in the east. After a few moments, she responded, "Father, Quacey and I came to live here when she married Stuart. Mama had just died, so it was the three of us. I think I was ten or eleven then. After Quacey disappeared, we just never left. Even though we didn't know where she had gone, I think Dad just felt closer to her here on the island."

"That must have been very hard on you at such a young age."

"I don't think I understood for a while," Lainie responded as her eyes began to tear up. "She was here one day, and the next she was gone. No note, no goodbye, no explanation. Nothing."

For a moment, Lainie sat in silence. To Elle, she looked perhaps twenty-four or twenty-five, although she knew her to be in her early thirties. Her blond hair was long and natural with just a touch of a strawberry undertone. Like her father, she had blue eyes that captivated. But while his sparkled with wit, Lainie's were tinged with melancholy. Whether she knew it or not, Lainie was beautiful.

"I'd probably have left years ago," Lainie said suddenly, surprising Elle. "But I have always worried about Father. He's not *of* Aldermire, but I feel he belongs here now. He's become a part of it, and if I leave, I'd have to leave him behind. Losing one daughter nearly killed him. I don't know that he'd survive losing a second."

12

And all the people saw the thunderings, and the lightnings, and the noise of the trumpet, and the mountain smoking: and when the people saw it, they removed, and stood afar off.

And they said unto Moses, Speak thou with us, and we will hear: but let not God speak with us, lest we die.

And Moses said unto the people, Fear not: for God is come to prove you, and that his fear may be before your faces, that ye sin not.

— Exodus 20: 18-20, *The King James Bible*

Elle helped to wash and store the blackberries. Lainie fed Angus a few raw carrots and checked the soup that was reheating on the stove. Lunch, she mentioned in apology, was going to be a few random leftovers from the past two days. To her dismay, Elle realized she herself never had meals, let alone leftovers, this good whether she was single or married. As much as she loved food, where it came from and how it got so tasty was, to Elle, still quite a mystery.

A large tureen of the finished soup was set in the dining room next to fresh flaky rolls and a green salad. From the front hall, Elle called the available family down for dinner. Megan and Cade were the only two to answer her summons.

While Lainie continued cleaning the day's harvest in the kitchen, the trio sat and ate in silence. As Elle picked at her soup, she thought about the voices she overheard in the white cottage. Given her suspicions, she knew she needed to cross and likely burn a very delicate bridge.

She looked from Megan to Cade, then back to Megan. The meal was delicious, but she had already lost her appetite. Suddenly Elle felt grateful they were having soup. A quick look revealed no forks, knives or anything else sharp within Megan's immediate reach. Just a spoon gave Elle a fighting chance.

She took a pair of deep breaths and played her hand.

"Megan, I don't want to upset you, but I need to ask Cade a difficult question."

Megan stopped mid-slurp, set her spoon down and gave Elle her full focus.

"You don't know when to quit," she said with considerable sarcasm. "Just when we were learning to get along."

Cade raised both hands. "Mom, it's fine. There's nothing I can't answer. Shoot."

Elle took another deep breath and backed her chair up a few inches. She tried to estimate her sprinting distance to the front door. She chose her next words with care.

"The night Stuart died, I heard a pair of voices in the white cottage," she began. "Megan, you yourself said that someone had moved the pillows on the bed. I've thought about this from every angle, and the only two people who could have been in the cottage were Cade and Lainie." Megan froze.

"Cade, this isn't easy," Elle continued, "but did you and Lainie come home early from Saint Andrews? Were you both in the cottage the night Stuart was killed?"

"Elle, don't you dare," Megan growled. "You leave my son out of this."

"Mom, I hate to say it, but she's right," he admitted. Megan turned to him and opened her mouth to speak, but she couldn't seem to find a word. Elle, too, was shocked. It had made perfect sense, but she had assumed—and hoped—she was wrong.

"Okay, let me rephrase that," he explained. "She's right on part of it. True, Lainie and I didn't spend all evening in Saint Andrews. I took us over in the boat, then I grabbed dinner with Deanne and Jerry. She went to the movies. Originally, I was going to pick her up after midnight at McGuire's on the dock. But she said she was getting a ride home right after the movie got out."

"Keep going," Megan insisted. Her rage was no longer focused on Elle, and Elle knew it was too good to last.

"If she didn't come over on the ferry, she could have gotten a ride from Anna or Felicia. Listen, at the time it didn't seem like a big deal. When Miss Mackay found Stuart, Lainie went nuts and told me to say we had come back together. I honestly didn't think it would matter."

"Cade, please tell me you weren't sleeping with Lainie," Megan asked, her eyes never leaving her son's.

"Mom, how many times have we talked about this? I'm not sleeping with anyone. Especially not Lainie."

"Why do you say that?" Elle asked.

"Okay, she's a nice person and all, but she's just not my type," he replied. "She's like twice my age. And I don't want to call her out, but I think she's a little off-center. I don't think she's, like, batshit insane or anything, but she's definitely a special kind of crazy."

"How special?" Megan asked.

"I don't know; it's like she's been here too long or something," he explained. "I think this place gets in your head, and it starts to scramble things. No matter what you try to talk to her about, it always comes back to this place. 'Hey, girl, what did you think about the movie?' 'Oh, it was fine, but we don't have giant space robots back on Aldermire.' It's like even when she leaves the island, some little part of her is still stuck here. It's seriously kinda creepy."

"Cade, you lied to the police," Megan said as she rubbed the sides of her head. "Do you have any idea how serious that is?"

"Mom, I'm sorry. I didn't think it was important. She just didn't want the MacUspaigs to know she'd come back early."

"If it helps, I can talk to Jonah," Elle offered. "Megan, I'm so sorry I even brought it up."

Ignoring Elle's suggestion, Megan handed Cade her bowl. "Take these to the kitchen, then head straight up to your room," she said. "We are going to have a long talk about the list of people you don't lie to. I'll give you a preview. I'm at the top of that list. The police are in the top five." She paused. "On second thought, just leave the bowls here. Go straight up. I'll be up in a few minutes. Cade, I raised you better than this."

"Mom, I'm sorry," he said. His expression suggested he was telling the truth. He pushed away from the table and crossed the library, heading for the front stairs.

Elle stood from her chair and collected her half-finished bowl of soup.

"Don't think for a second I'm done with you," Megan said.

"Like I said, I'm so sorry I even brought it up," Elle repeated.

"I just have one question. Why now?"

"What do you mean?" The question caught Elle off guard.

"Forget it. Are you going to call Tanner or should I?" Megan asked with resignation.

"I'll be back in Saint Andrews tomorrow," Elle offered. "I can talk to him in person. I just don't see it being as bad for Cade as you think."

"Cade doesn't need to know that. He needs to sit and worry about this for a while longer."

Elle was about to respond when voices from the great hall cut her off. Lyle and Caroline entered through the library in the middle of a heated conversation, as they often were. They stopped short when they noticed the two women and the hot meal that waited for them.

"Soup again?" Caroline asked. "I'd say that Lainie is slipping. She had nothing else to do today, and this is what we get for lunch?" She gave an audible sigh in exaggerated exasperation.

Neither Elle nor Megan offered a greeting as the two new arrivals ladled bowls of the savory chicken soup. Caroline took a chair between the women and Lyle sat at the far end of the table.

"What is it with this house today?" she continued. "First Cade looks like someone shot his dog, and now you two are sharing soup under a little black cloud."

"It's been a *long* day," Megan replied, her tone clearly a warning and not an invitation to dig deeper. Caroline missed the implication entirely.

"What did the police want to talk with you about?" Caroline persisted.

"Just a few more questions about Stuart's body," Elle lied.

"And we're trying to figure out who was where and when," Megan added.

"Well, I think we were all pretty clear on that," Caroline responded.

"Not entirely," Elle replied in a hushed tone. "While Stuart was visiting me in the red cabin that night, I heard a pair of voices in the white cabin. I think we are fairly certain that one of them was Lainie."

"But wasn't she on the island with Cade?" Caroline asked with a mix of shock and curiosity.

"It turns out she wasn't. She came back a little early. The thing is, I can't figure out who else was with her."

"Well, it wasn't me, and Leith and Hendry were upstairs together," Caroline said, clearly enjoying the chance to gossip.

"It wasn't either of us," Elle continued as she considered the options, "and Cade was still in Saint Andrews. That only leaves..." As she formed the thought, she regretted her words. She looked up in time to see Lyle and Caroline lock eyes, both mouths agape. She dropped her own eyes back to her soup.

Damn, she thought just as Caroline's glass shattered into a thousand pieces on the wall behind Lyle's head.

Without a word, Caroline bolted from the dining room, Lyle in pursuit. After a few moments of silence, Elle looked up. Megan was staring at her in shock.

"Did that just happen?" the other woman asked in disbelief.

Failing to find the right words, Elle nodded, then shook her head. They sat in silence for a few more seconds.

"Holy crap. I always thought it would be me throwing the glass," she said, "and at you." In a whisper she added, "Um, well, should someone tell Lainie?"

"I think she may already know," Elle replied, one finger pointing at the kitchen door. Megan just covered her mouth and shook her head.

"Okay, I've had enough excitement for one day. Hell, I've had enough for one lifetime," Megan said. "I have to go check on Cade. If I were you, I'd find myself another hidden tunnel, fast."

As Megan left through the library, Elle sat at the empty table, slowly rubbing her temples.

"Think, then speak," she repeated to herself. It never ceased to amaze her how critical a half second of reflection could be. Over the past year, she had focused on developing an internal monologue, that split moment between the thought forming and words escaping her mouth. The longer that moment, the fewer headaches she created for herself.

Slipping away from the table, Elle checked the library, then the front hall with care. With no sign of any MacUspaig or Daleroch, she crept up the stairs and into her room. Just a few minutes past one o'clock, and the light through the tall windows was already beginning to dim. The storm hadn't yet arrived, but it was clearly on its way.

She shut the door and stood in the center of the room assessing the job ahead of her. After a few minutes of silence, she pulled her overnight case from the closet. She was haphazardly piling in layers of unwashed clothes when someone banged on the bedroom door.

Lyle's voice demanded something she couldn't quite make out, so Elle took her time with his request. After a few moments, she opened the bedroom door to find the younger MacUspaig just outside in the hall.

"It wasn't locked," she said, turning back to her packing.

"I don't know who the hell you think you are, but you are gone," he said with a naked rage. "This is my house, my family and my life. I want you the hell off Roan first thing in the morning."

"Way ahead of you, Lyle," she replied, looking back. "I think I have everything I need, so I plan on finishing my research in Saint Andrews."

"To hell with your research. With Stuart's death, the past few days have been a nightmare for me. The last thing I need is you stumbling around destroying more lives."

"Destroying lives?" Elle snapped back. Although she wasn't done packing, Elle slammed the case closed for dramatic effect. "All I did was ask the same questions the police would be asking later. You should be thanking me that you're figuring out your excuses now and not while sitting in front of Tanner. And another thing, I didn't destroy your life. I didn't hold a gun to your head and force you into the cottage with Lainie. That's your own damn fault. Don't you dare blame me if you can't keep it in your pants."

"If you're not out before lunch tomorrow, I'm calling the police," he replied. He left without waiting for her response.

Elle closed the door behind him and sat next to her overnight case. Emotionally drained, she fell back on the bed and looked up at the ceiling. In the fading light, the room appeared cavernous, the walls receding past her field of vision. This was not how she pictured her last day on Roan Island. In truth, she was already regretting the extra night at Aldermire.

Elle opened her eyes as a second, softer knock came at the bedroom door. The sunlight had suddenly shifted its position, and Elle guessed she may have napped for several minutes.

"It's open, come on in," she called without getting up from where she lay.

Elle heard the door open and close, but no one spoke. She sat up and found Lainie standing next to the bedroom door avoiding eye contact. Her faithful hound had reclaimed the oriental rug and was circling to find the perfect spot for a nap. As the young woman shifted her weight from one foot to the other, she clasped her hands tightly before her.

"Lainie, I don't know what to say," Elle said, if only to break the silence.

"Elle, I wanted to apologize for Lyle. He can be difficult to talk to when he's angry."

"You have nothing to apologize for," Elle replied. "You two did whatever you two did, and it's none of my business. You all are adults, and I should have kept my mouth shut."

Lainie crossed the room and sat on the foot of the bed. She still wasn't making eye contact, but Elle guessed she had been crying.

"There's just a couple of things I wanted you to know," Lainie continued as she struggled to find words. "This is so much more than just that one night. Lyle and I have been together on and off since he was in college. One summer he actually proposed to me. It was the most magical day of my life; it was like a fairy tale.

"He told his father, and Hendry forbade it," she said, then paused for several seconds. "He refused to let Lyle marry me, said I was too old, not the kind of wife his son deserved. Lyle fought back, but Hendry threatened to throw us both off the estate. It was Stuart's decision to make, but Hendry still held this house with an iron hand."

"I'm so sorry to hear that," Elle said. Lainie shrugged.

"He said he needed to move on, so he went back to college and then up and married Caroline," she continued. "I guess they were happy, but I don't think she has ever loved him. Not like I did. Honestly, I don't know if she even knows we were engaged."

"Lainie, how do you live here with them both?" Elle asked. "Why stay at Aldermire all these years?"

"This is my home," she replied as the tears began to fall. "And I've come to terms with it. I've forgiven Hendry, and I've forgiven Lyle. My only options were to live at Aldermire with him or live somewhere else without him. I made my choice."

After Lainie had said her piece and left, the first rain began to fall. Water ran down the old glass panes in rivers as the afternoon sun disappeared from view. Elle turned on the bedside lamp and tried to focus on packing. Without the sunlight, the room took on a sudden chill, and Elle picked up her pace to stay warm.

As she sorted the last few notes she had carried over to the great house, the sound of the rain was again broken by a knock on the door. Elle groaned.

"Come in. I'm leaving it unlocked."

The door opened slightly, and Megan MacUspaig asked, "Do you have a minute?" Elle had no response. She sat on the bed, mouth open, unsure how to reply.

Megan stepped into the room and showed both hands. "I'm unarmed, if it helps. Want to pat me down, just in case?"

"Uh, no, it's fine. Turns out I'm popular this afternoon."

Megan made it halfway into the room before she stopped. "Can we talk without the daggers?"

Elle thought for a moment. "Well, you clearly don't like me, and I've developed a very healthy fear of you. That seems to be working for us. Why mess with a good thing?"

Megan rolled her eyes and sighed. "Actually, I wanted to apologize."

"What? Wait. Really?"

"Don't make this any harder than it has to be. I just want to keep it short and simple."

"Short? Girl, I've got all night," Elle said with a wicked smile.

"I'm just going to get this out. Don't interrupt me, deal?"

Elle nodded, still smiling.

"Okay, two things. First, I have no idea why you did it, but thank you for telling Tanner that I wasn't involved with Stuart's death. I don't know if he believed you, but that was way above and beyond."

"I honestly didn't think..."

"Don't interrupt. The second one is more of a question, maybe followed by an apology," Megan continued.

"Alright, shoot."

"An hour ago you cornered Cade on the lie he told the police about when he and Lainie came back to Aldermire. When did that little brainstorm happen?"

"Last night when I couldn't sleep," Elle replied. "To me it made..."

"Still interrupting. If you knew about it last night, why not say something to the cops when they were here this morning? You could have just told Tanner and let them figure it out."

Elle sat still, not responding. After a few seconds, she replied, "Can I answer now or is it still interrupting?"

"The floor is all yours."

"Honestly, I was pretty sure I was right—or, as it turns out, at least half right," Elle continued. "If I was wrong, I didn't want to risk stringing him up like that. He seems like a good guy. Actually, I was kind of hoping I was wrong."

Megan stood looking down at Elle for several seconds.

"Thank you for that," she said at last. "And I apologize if I perhaps came on a little strong. Mess with me, and I'm fine. I can take care of myself. Mess with my son, and I'll take you down."

"I can respect that," Elle said. "I know all about strong mothers. He's lucky to have a parent like you. So, Megan, can I ask you a question?"

"No guarantee I'll answer, but you can ask if you want," she replied.

"You've made it clear you don't want me here, even before Stuart's death," Elle noted. "I'd like to know why. We barely knew each other in high school, and anything that happened between Stuart and me happened long before you all married, before you even dated."

Megan appeared to be considering Elle's request and nodded. "I guess I owe you that." She paused again. "Honestly, I have no idea. I've been angry at you since the day you arrived. Just knowing that you had been with Stuart in the past stuck in my craw. I couldn't move past it."

"Did you think we were sneaking around behind your back?" Elle asked.

"I never saw that happening," Megan admitted. "That's the crazy part. I was more worried about him sleeping with Lainie. One time he mentioned how much she reminded him of her sister. I can only assume that they are similar, as you'll be damned to find a picture of Quacey anywhere in the house. After she died, it was like the MacUspaigs had her spirit exorcised from Aldermire. And, more than that, I figured you were too smart to let Stuart try anything."

Elle laughed out loud. "Too smart? That's not one I hear very often."

"If anything, that's what pissed me off more," Megan continued.

"How'd that piss you off?"

Megan thought again and sighed. "Listen, you were first, and I was second. I was okay with that. When I met Stuart, he made me feel like the most important, beautiful woman in the world. The sun rose and set over me and only me."

"I know how that feels," Elle noted. Megan chuckled.

"Exactly," she said. "You do know how that feels. You were in the exact same place I was: single, sleeping with Stuart and basking in his bullshit."

"So why does that make you angry with me?" Elle asked.

"You were smarter than I was," she replied. "I fell for his bullshit, and you saw through it. Every compliment and every lie—after my first marriage, I just couldn't get enough of that kind of attention. By the time I realized what an ass he was, I was stuck here on this damn island. You, on the other hand, were smart enough to take the goods and leave him hanging. I still resent that. And I think that's what pisses me off so much."

"Well don't pat me on the back so soon," Elle commented. "Not marrying Stuart—and he did ask—was the one good decision I made that year. Probably the next two or three years, too. Megan, whatever you may think, you are still miles ahead of me."

"I heard from Bea that you had gotten married, too," Megan said.

"Oh, that's a long story." Elle tried to dodge the subject.

"As I think you said, 'Girl, I've got all night.'"

Elle shrugged. "Well, I married Dan about six years ago. We had been friends throughout college, and when he got a divorce from his first wife, we kinda picked up where we left off. It was a bad match from the start. I had my post-grad work;

he had the whole work thing. Honestly, I spent more time with his daughter than I did with him. Last year I found out he was sleeping with this woman Tammy, one of the other athletes from the Highland games we'd attend."

"You don't sound too broken up about it," Megan noted.

"Well, we never saw each other," Elle said and sighed. "We were still married, but we simply lost touch. I can't count the number of times I thought about walking out or maybe finding someone else. He just beat me to the punch. In my heart I know I shouldn't blame him." She paused and reconsidered. "Scratch that. I should blame him. And I do. A lot. Maybe I feel I should share some of that blame with him. But at the end of the day, he screwed up."

"No, he screwed Tammy," Megan said a cackle. "Listen, we've both been married. We've both thought about leaving, about being with another man, about starting over with someone new and exciting. It's a part of marriage. Another part of marriage is not acting on it. If it's right, work on it. If it's not right, get a divorce. Don't screw around behind your wife's back. Not to pry, but how'd you find out about Tammy?"

Elle rolled her eyes. "We were at the games in Charlotte, and Dan was running late. I drove back to the hotel to pick him up, and he comes jogging through the lobby with Tammy looking a little flushed."

"No crime in that."

"Yeah, but they were wearing each other's sports kilts," Elle replied. "Never rush to get dressed in the dark. While he was blustering about and trying to explain, I did a caber toss off the hotel balcony with his suitcase and gear. I moved out two days later, and we were divorced within a month."

"I never had the luxury of catching Stuart at it," Megan replied.

"I don't know that it made it any easier, but it certainly put a quick end to our misery."

"Why'd you keep his last name?"

Elle groaned and lay back on the bed. "Paperwork. I know it should take all of an hour, but I just never got around to changing it back. The first few weeks after we split were a blur. That was followed by a few months I'll just call 'hazy.' By the time I found my footing, it just didn't seem important. It's a lousy answer, but it's the truth."

"Are you still in touch?" Megan asked.

"More so recently," Elle replied. "Despite what my mother might say, he's not a monster. We just didn't fit back then. He's still a good friend, and I'm crazy about his daughter, Paige. She's bold and creative and strong. She's amazing. Since last summer, I've been taking her out for lunch now and then, a couple of girl days shopping or helping her build chicken coops." Megan gave her an odd look. "Don't ask. That's her thing this year. Last year it was welding. I am so much happier with the chickens."

"Sounds like a neat kid," Megan said with a smile.

"She's a rock star. Maybe if I stick around some of that will rub off on me. Or maybe I can inspire her."

"If only as a cautionary example," she replied. Elle shot her a half-hearted dirty look.

"Ha ha. Okay, one more question for you," Elle said. "Where in the hell did you learn Latin?" Megan laughed.

"Remember senior year when I switched schools?"

"Vaguely."

"My parents were divorcing, I ended up at a Catholic finishing school for girls. One of those places that focused on the classics, like Latin. But their big goal was teaching me to be charming and sophisticated. It didn't work," Megan concluded.

For several minutes Megan sat in a chair looking out at the pouring rain as Elle continued her packing. The newly widowed Mrs. MacUspaig broke the silence by clearing her throat.

"Okay, I have to ask," she said. "Given your checkered history with my husband, why the burning desire to find out who killed him?"

Elle had asked herself the same question more than once. "Listen, we can both agree that Stuart was a grade-A, whiskey-soaked, tartan-kilted jackass. But as much of an ass as he was, he didn't deserve what he got. Nothing he did to either one of us would ever warrant being stabbed in the back and left to die."

Megan nodded. "Personally, I would have preferred something less lethal and more humiliating."

"Someone else didn't agree," Elle replied. "That's what scares me. One of us was willing to kill Stuart, and that's a huge risk. Aren't you the least bit curious? Or at the very least, worried?"

"If I am worried, it's more for my son than for me. And how do you know I didn't do it?"

"Stabbing him in the back isn't your style," Elle replied. "I told Jonah that if you had wanted Stuart dead, you'd have done it with spotlights and a jazz band. It would have been choreographed and set to music."

Megan nodded again. "That has a certain flair. Much more my style."

"I've been in your shoes, and my guess is you were already set to move on," Elle added. "Why kill him when you already had one foot out the door?"

"Divorce was definitely on the table, but we hadn't made any concrete plans," Megan continued. "The prenup made it all pretty cut and dry. I just wanted to talk to Cade first, find some place we could settle for a while. All this drama about selling Aldermire and leaving the island? That was news to me. In any case, thank you for the benefit of the doubt."

Elle closed her overnight bag and took the seat across from Megan. "So how do you know I didn't do it?"

"First, what did you possibly have to gain from killing him?" Megan replied. "I could only assume that you were in the wrong place at the wrong time. And I am taking your word that nothing at all happened between you that night."

Elle raised her right hand. "I swear on my dear mother's life. When I was younger, Stuart was a fling—a magnetic, charming, scandalous fling. Life is different now. I'm getting my shit together, and Stuart never facilitated that kind of self-improvement. More important, he is...was married. I've been on both ends of that knife through the heart. I wouldn't do that to myself, and I wouldn't do that to you."

Megan regarded Elle for an uncomfortable second. "Despite my long-standing urge to toss you from a window and dance on your grave, I believe you."

Elle smiled. "Want a hug?"

"No."

"You sure?"

"Quite."

Megan adjusted herself in the chair.

"Second," she continued as she leaned into Elle, "there were no tire tracks across his back."

"You heard about that?"

It was Megan's turn to smile. "Darling, we *all* heard about that. And something tells me there's far more to the story."

"Let's save it for another confessional."

"Not a chance. Start talking."

Elle raised her hands in surrender. "After I caught Dan with Tammy, I *might* have had a few drinks. I *might* have used my truck to ram Tammy's hatchback out of a parking space and into a ditch. And she and Dan *might* have been in the back seat of the car at the time. I say 'might' under the advice of my lawyer. Got a stern lecture from the judge, a lot of community service but no hard time in the big house. Just a week in county lockup for mouthing off in court. I'll spare you that part of the story today."

Megan let loose with a hearty guffaw. "I knew there had to be something about you I liked. Gotta be careful with that temper, girl."

"You say temper; I say a flair for theatrical justice."

"So why her car?" Megan asked.

"Why not?"

"That has always stumped me," Megan answered. "When a husband cheats, why does the wife always go after the other woman? Shouldn't she be angry at her husband?"

"Says the woman who's been holding a grudge against me for sleeping with her husband long before he was her husband."

Megan looked back to the rain outside. "Don't get me wrong; I can be pissed at the two of you. And I'm still on the fence."

"About what?"

Megan shrugged. "Not sure which I would enjoy more, liking you or hating you."

"Why not both?"

"So what the hell do you think is going on here?" Megan asked. "I've gone over it in my head a hundred times, and I can't make sense of Stuart's murder. He was a jackass, but why would anyone want him dead?"

"Your guess is as good as mine," Elle replied.

"Another thing. I know you dodged the police on Lainie coming back early. Anything else you forgot to mention?"

Elle thought for a minute, then stood up and walked over to her laptop bag. She fished around and pulled out a slip of white paper with red, blocky writing. She handed it to Megan.

"Actually, until you asked, I had completely forgotten about this."

"Where did you find this?" Megan asked as she flipped it over.

"It was on the floor where Stuart had left his sporran that night."

"'You have broken the fifth.' What kind of nonsense is this? The fifth of what?" Megan asked.

"Well, the fifth could be a date, a promise, maybe a fifth of scotch."

"Well, breaking a fifth of scotch *could* get you killed around here."

"My money is on a commandment," Elle replied.

"That would be my guess, too. 'Thou shalt not kill.' That year at Catholic school is really paying off this week. The only person who may have been killed on Aldermire that I know of, Stuart excluded, is Quacey, and that was however many years ago."

Elle retrieved the small slip of paper. "But how does Stuart link to Quacey's death? Everything I've heard is that he was in Richmond when she disappeared. So why threaten him now?

And why kill him over something that no one believes he could have done?"

"Since we're being all friendly-like, I'll up you one better," Megan said with a furrowed brow. "This note might tie in with something else from yesterday."

"You have my complete attention."

"Last night, Caroline and I were talking in the library after dinner," Megan recalled. "She was still prattling on about something, probably that nonexistent treasure, and she finally said something of interest. While taking off her rain gear yesterday, she found a note on Lyle's dresser. She didn't get a chance to see it, but she did mention white paper and red ink."

"Oh, my God," Elle replied. "What did it say?"

"Something about 'We need to meet tonight' or something similar," Megan said. "After this morning, I assumed it was something to do with Lainie. But even that doesn't make sense, because she was going to be in Saint Andrews with us last night."

"That's assuming he had gotten the note yesterday. And 'tonight' is a pretty wide spread," Elle noted. "It could have been after dinner or after midnight."

"True, but I thought it's something to think about."

"No, you are definitely on to something. I just don't know what any of it means."

"Speaking of Caroline, what do you think about that treasure?" Megan asked.

"I can't believe she's still talking about that."

Megan shook her head. "Never shut up about it. I'm surprised she hasn't spent the day digging holes in the basement."

"I don't know," Elle said and thought for a moment. "It may be something, but I'd like to hear about it from someone else first. She doesn't really hit me as the most reliable expert on what you might find buried under Aldermire." Elle gave Megan a serious look. "So, in the interest of being charming, can we call a peace?"

Megan shrugged.

"A temporary truce?" Elle offered.

Megan shrugged again.

Elle tried again, "How about a momentary cease fire so we can collect our dead and wounded?"

"I can go for that."

13

The best revenge is to be unlike him who performed the injury.

— Marcus Aurelius, *Meditations*

Despite her appetite, Elle had no interest in sitting down to a meal with the family. Lainie had called for dinner at 7 p.m. promptly. At five minutes to seven, Elle was still considering her options. After two more minutes of careful deliberation, she let hunger win, and she stepped into the upstairs hall.

She walked the length of the hallway, planning to take the back stairs through the kitchen. Food left out on the counter might be enough to hold her until morning.

As she passed the grand French doors granting access to the second-floor balcony, the tableau took her breath away. The sky was a patchwork of deep thunderhead purples and sunset reds. Flashes of lightning arced through the clouds and lit the ground of Roan Island beneath her.

She opened the center door, and her senses were piqued by the damp chill in the air and the electric scent of ozone. Beyond the alder trees, the river was a void. Even the occasional streak of lighting found nothing to highlight. To Elle, it looked and felt like the world ended on Roan's rain-lashed shore.

Elle stepped onto the patio, the permanent canopy protecting her from the worst of the deluge now soaking the island. In the feeble estate lights, she could make out the house's namesake trees, the terrace below, Lainie's prized gardens, the cottages huddled in the distance and little more. She approached the balcony's railing and braced herself against one of the large planters that overflowed with holly and coral beauty.

Even obscured by the dim light and wavering sheets of rain, Elle could sense the majesty of this island home. For more than fifty years, Hendry had served as the lord of the manor, despite any title or deed granted his sons. Standing here, she could understand his pride and vanity. In its isolation and its beauty, Roan was a kingdom truly fit for a king.

A bolt of lightning flashed just overhead, the sudden roll of thunder snapping Elle from her thoughts. She stepped back from the balcony, tucked a few stray curls behind her ears and chose the front stairs to join the family for dinner.

Arriving a few minutes after seven, Elle found the rest of the group already seated and passing plates of food. Lainie brought in a small platter of steamed cauliflower to complement the salmon fillets. As she set the side dish down, Elle noticed the young woman lock eyes with Lyle, if only for a brief moment. Lainie declined her father's offer to join them at the table, feigning a need to work in the kitchen before turning in early.

Hendry and Leith had taken up at each end of the long table, while Megan and Cade sat together on one side. Lyle sat alone, glowering at the food in front of him. Elle wasn't sure if his awkward revelation had yet reached either patriarch's ear, although the young MacUspaig's mood suggested he knew it soon might. Elle took the seat next to Megan, who regarded her with a newfound sense of tacit comradery.

"I don't think Caroline is joining us tonight," Megan whispered in Elle's ear. "Lainie begged off, too. Even so, dinner should be more awkward than usual."

She hit a bullseye with that one, Elle later thought. Even Leith, usually a reliable source of conversation and conviviality, was quiet during the meal. Although there was no dessert, Lainie provided the table with an after-dinner wine. It wasn't to Elle's tastes, but it helped loosen the mood around the table.

Lyle looked up from his food long enough to inform the group that he was leaving Aldermire in the morning, possibly for a week or more. Leith set down his wine and shook his head.

"Do you really think now is the time to be traveling?" the older man asked. "I do understand your desire to be free of this island, if only for a few days, but I don't think we're finished here."

"And we still need to take care of the arrangements for Stuart," Megan noted. "I'd do it, but I have no idea where to start."

Hendry gave his signature harsh laugh, cutting off Megan's words. "After all this time, you choose now to worry about how to pay tribute to your husband. Miserable woman."

"Hendry, that's uncalled for," Leith interjected.

"Hold your tongue, Daleroch," the MacUspaig patriarch growled. "For three years she spat on the MacUspaig family, not surprising given her upbringing. Now that he's dead, she shows some shred of remorse. I say let her rot and live with what she's done to our clan's good name. The torture of a bad conscience is the hell of a living soul."

Cade began to speak, but Megan took his hand and squeezed a preemptive warning.

"Old man, I'm sure it will delight you to know that we are leaving Aldermire as well," she said at last. "This has never felt like home, so no need to outstay my welcome any more than I already have."

Lyle looked at Elle for the first time since the meal began and said, "And based on our conversation from earlier, Elle is out too. She'll be gone before lunch. Should be a quiet few days around the island." Lyle drummed his fingers on the table. "I'm beginning to think Stuart may have had the start of a good idea. When I come back, we'll be making some changes around here. For the one or two of you who may not already know, Caroline and I are at a crossroads. No idea where it might lead. I'll deal with her later.

"For the rest of you, it's time for some new blood at Aldermire. Elle, as we've already discussed, I want you off Roan by lunch tomorrow. Megan, let me know what you plan on leaving with. If I have any concerns, we will work them out before anything is taken off island. Leith, you and Lainie are like family, but you all need to make a new start. Take until the end of the month to find a new home.

"And Dad, according to what Leith and MacFarlane have explained to me, it's clear that Aldermire is mine. You're free to stay here as you like, but I'll be running the house from here on out."

Megan laughed and raised her glass. "To the new lord of Aldermire," she said. "Sounds like it's gonna be awfully lonely here on Roan. So, Lyle, what's the good of being king when there aren't any peasants to lord over? Had you asked him, Stuart could have given you an earful."

"You're more like your brother than I gave you credit for," Hendry said with a harsh smile. "You want the crown? Consider it yours, and with it all the trappings of this sacred place. But with riches comes responsibility, for nothing is more dangerous than to be blinded by prosperity. Just be prepared to carry on the good MacUspaig name."

Leith stood from his chair and looked at each member of the family in turn before speaking. "More than once in my life, I have been accused of wearing my heart upon my sleeve 'for daws to peck at,' as Shakespeare would say. Thus, I feel I must speak my mind plainly.

"Lyle, it saddens me to see you following in your brother's footsteps, but perhaps it's something native to the MacUspaig blood. Now, please excuse me. I should check on Lainie and let her know that our lives might be changing sooner than we had thought."

As the Daleroch patriarch made his way to the kitchen, Hendry MacUspaig stood from his chair at the head of the table.

"It appears that the storm outside Aldermire pales in comparison to the tempest stirring within her halls," he said. "If anyone needs to speak with me, which will be both unlikely and unwelcome, I'll be in my study." Without acknowledging his son or the other guests, he left the table and walked through the library to the front stairs.

"Well, this really has been a delight," Lyle said with a growl. "I'm sure this is a dinner I'll remember for a very long time. Ladies, it's been a pleasure having you as guests here at Aldermire. Your absence from my life will certainly be noted."

"Jackass," Cade said under his breath. As the new lord of Aldermire left the table, his only response to the insult was a condescending smile.

"I'm out of here," Cade said at last. "Love you, Mom." He gave Megan a hug and took the back stairs toward his room. The two women sat in silence for a moment as the wind and thunder raged outside the dining room windows.

"My guess is that Lyle will be looking for somewhere else to sleep tonight," Elle said, finishing off the glass of overly sweet German wine.

"Shame you aren't still in the red cottage tonight," Megan responded. "Seems to be a popular choice for secondhand husbands."

Elle shot her a surprised look.

Megan held up her palms in peace. "Sorry, Elle, old habits," she said with a shrug.

"You owe me one," Elle replied with a wicked side eye. "So do you think we're all done with the drama for the night?"

As the last word escaped her lips, the lights throughout the house snapped off. Through the windows, it was clear that the estate lights had also been extinguished. The two women sat in complete darkness as occasional flashes of lightning briefly lit the world around them. There was no sound, no sights, only the storm.

Megan whispered to Elle, "Well, that was stupid question."

"Mom?" Cade's voice called from beyond the dining room. A few moments later an oval of light bobbed down the front stairs and across the library. He bolted through the connecting door, holding a signal-less cell phone for illumination and still calling for Megan.

"Honey, I'm fine," she responded. "Elle and I are here. Did you see anyone else?"

"No, I was getting ready for bed and everything went dark."

"Hello?" Caroline called as she and Lainie entered from opposite ends of the room. Lyle followed Lainie by only a few seconds.

"Is everyone okay?" he asked, casting a flashlight beam around the room.

"We are just missing Hendry and Leith," Elle noted. From her pocket, Lainie produced a small lighter and began to light the ornamental candles in the table's centerpiece.

After a short debate, Cade and Lainie were selected to check on the elder pair while the rest congregated in the dining room. As the pair exited through the library, another voice was heard coming from the kitchen.

"Consider us accounted for," Leith called out. He entered from the kitchen, leading Hendry by the hand. The two men took chairs at the head of the table, glancing around the room in the candlelight.

"Well, that's everyone," Megan noted. "Any idea what happened?"

"Probably just the storm," Lyle answered. "If a line goes down, it takes out the entire island. And if the storm is big enough, Roan is usually one of the last lines they bring back up. We could be out for a while."

"The only thing less enjoyable than spending the evening with this miserable lot is spending the evening with this miserable lot in the dark," Hendry said to no one in particular.

Leith shook his head. "I'll make sure Hendry makes it back to his study. Does everyone else have a light?" he asked.

"There are more flashlights and candles in the kitchen," Lainie noted as she stepped from the room. She quickly returned with a small tub of extra lights.

"Thank you, my dear," Leith said as he kissed his daughter's forehead. He began passing out the supplies to each of the family members. "It may be a long night, so we may want to turn in early."

"I guess I'll be back in my room," Lainie said.

"I'll be in *my* room," Caroline echoed, staring daggers at the other woman.

Elle reached out and squeezed Megan's hand. "We're going to grab a drink in the kitchen, then head upstairs to our rooms and check on Angus," she said.

"Cade, honey, head upstairs," Megan said to her son. "Lock the door," she whispered.

"I have no idea if it will work, but I'm going to take the front path to the pump house," Lyle said. "The old generator is in there, and with some gas from the boathouse, it could at least get us a few lights on until the crews finish their work. God only knows when that will be."

Caroline raised a hand as though to caution him, then looked back at Lainie and perhaps thought better of it. She and Cade left together through the library as Lyle made his way to the front hall. Leith and Lainie escorted Hendry out through the kitchen and up to his private study.

"Okay, what the hell was that?" Megan asked once the two women were alone.

"Just a quick trip to check an idea I had," Elle explained. "I want to see if I'm right. Grab one of those flashlights. Actually, grab two."

"And you needed me for this because?"

"Right or wrong, I figured there's safety in numbers," she replied with a grin. "Having you around doubles my chances."

The old servants' dining room sat as it had for years, a storage space for those things too bulky to drag down to the basement. Even with flashlights, Elle and Megan took care navigating the tiny space.

To her surprise, Elle found the door to the back coatroom ajar. She shone the beam through the door and onto the recessed panel just beyond. With her free hand, she reached into the small closet and pushed the makeshift door, revealing the pitch-black expanse of the basement below.

"Like hell I'm going in there," Megan said.

"I thought you went looking for me in the basement yesterday," Elle said.

"Ha! No, that was Caroline and Lainie. They tried the basement," she replied. "I did a very thorough search of my bedroom, then the hall outside my bedroom, then my bedroom again. Just in case you doubled back." Megan gave an exaggerated smile. "Because I knew you'd have done the same for me," she added sweetly.

Elle laughed despite herself. "Okay, I'll go first." Then she added, "Just a friendly word of advice: stay away from any open tunnel doors."

"Check."

They descended the stairs together. When they reached the basement, Elle shone her light on the wall to her left. She gave an audible gasp.

"Damn," she exclaimed. The main circuit breakers all had been pulled from the wall panel. Several other smaller breakers were missing as well. Elle scoured the floor with the beam of her flashlight, but her search yielded nothing of use.

"Please, God, don't tell me that someone did this on purpose," Megan whispered. Even in the ambient glow of the flashlight, Elle could see that most of the color had faded from the other woman's face. "We need to get the hell out of here."

"Cade, honey?" She knocked again, this time louder. Megan's voice was becoming tinged with panic. She tried the doorknob and, as she had requested, the door to her son's room was locked. With an open palm, she banged against the solid wood, the drum beat of the pounding blending with the constant roll of thunder outside.

As Megan tried the knob a second time, Elle heard the lock turn and the door inch open. Cade stood just inside his room, a pair of headphones covering each side of his head. He slid them off his ears until they rested around his neck. To Elle, he looked as though he may have been dozing.

"Oh, thank God, honey," Megan whispered with relief. She pushed the door open and gave her son a vice-like hug. Her obvious fear caught Cade off guard.

"Mom, I'm fine," he protested. "What's wrong?"

"Long story," Elle replied. "Someone cut the power on purpose. We're just not sure who or why. We need to make a call to the police, but your mom wanted to stop here first."

"Cade, put some shoes on," Megan said. "You are staying with me until this whole thing is over. You don't leave me for a second. Understand?"

Cade nodded and sat on the edge of his mattress. He kicked his running shoes out from beneath the bed and was soon ready to go. As he joined Elle and Megan at the door, women's voices could be heard echoing down the hall.

"Caroline doesn't sound happy," Megan observed, then shook her head. "Lainie's on her own until I know the police are on the way."

"Where's the closest landline?" Elle asked.

"In the main house, just the one on the back upstairs landing and one in Stuart's office downstairs. Hendry hated the things, but Stuart and Leith insisted. They compromised."

The trio made their way down the long hall toward the back stairs. As they passed Lainie's room, the women's voices rose to a crescendo. Elle considered intervening but Megan's hand gripping her own forced the decision. At the rear landing, Megan shone her flashlight on a small stand next to an overstuffed chair.

"Damn, damn, damn," Elle whispered. The small stand, where the phone had sat just the night before, was empty.

"Why cut the lines when you can take the whole damn phone?" Megan muttered. "Should we check the office, too, or would whoever's doing this be happy with just the one phone?"

"Okay, that's it," Elle said after a moment of thought. "Since dinner, this has gone from creepy to dangerous. Let's get everyone together, and this time, no one leaves the room until morning."

"I'm guessing Leith and Hendry are in his study," Megan noted. "And I think we know where Caroline and Lainie are. That just leaves Lyle."

"He's been gone for maybe thirty minutes? And if he made it to the pump house, whatever he tried hasn't worked," Elle replied.

"Do you think we could make it to either Old Town or Wilmington by boat?" Cade asked. The women considered the idea.

"It's not far from the west edge to the east bank, maybe 1,500 feet, but there's nothing there but marsh," she replied. "To get to a phone, we'd need to go north and over to Wilmington. Maybe a mile or more."

"It's not the distance that worries me," Elle interjected. "In this storm we wouldn't make it fifty feet. I can't believe I'm saying this, but we're probably safer on Roan than in the boat. Well, at least until the wind dies down a little."

"I hate to admit it, but you're probably right," Megan replied. "Let's gather everyone together in one room and figure that out when the storm slows."

As they made their way back down the upstairs hallway, the women's voices continued to rise and fall. They approached Lainie's bedroom, and before Elle could knock, the door flew open and Caroline burst into the hallway, nearly knocking Elle off her feet.

As she stared at the three interlopers, her rage was palpable. Far beyond her, Lainie stood at the window of her room, avoiding eye contact with the group.

"Where the hell is Lyle?" Caroline growled. "I need to speak to him *now*."

"Caroline, we haven't seen him since he left," Elle replied. "As far as we know, he hasn't come back from the pump house."

At the mention of Lyle's absence, his wife's anger broke. Over the course of a fleeting moment, her rage melted into concern, then fear.

"We need to find him," she exclaimed.

"Well, it gets worse," Elle said, "and Lainie, you should hear this, too." She took a deep breath and continued, "The storm didn't take the lights out. Someone deliberately cut the power to the house. We just checked, and the upstairs landline phone is missing, too."

"Oh, God," Caroline gasped as she brought her hands to her mouth. "What the hell is going on?"

"We don't know, but we think it's safer if we all just stay together until morning comes or we can get the boat off the island."

Their bitter rivalry apparently forgotten, Lainie and Caroline were quick to join the others in the hallway. As a group, they made their way to Hendry's private study. The door was closed but unlocked. Elle knocked and turned the knob without waiting for a response.

The two men were seated, motionless, in massive library chairs in front of the fireplace. The burning embers gave the study warmth and life despite the sinister shadows the firelight cast around the room.

Elle approached the pair, and Leith's eyes flicked up to meet hers. He gave a small jump, then smiled. "My dear, you shouldn't creep up on old men like that," he said with a weary laugh. "We didn't hear you come in. Care to join us in a drink?" He lifted his tumbler of whiskey and gave it a playful shake.

"We haven't seen Lyle since he left for the pump house," she said softly. Her words provoked an immediate response from Hendry as he sat upright in the massive chair.

"What the hell do you mean?" he demanded. "What have you done with my boy?" He pointed an accusatory finger at Caroline, then fell back into his chair.

"Hendry, we are going to find him," she replied. "At this point, we just think there is safety in numbers."

"If you all want to search for him," Leith suggested, "I can keep Hendry company."

Elle nodded. "That would be good. Lainie and Caroline, why don't you two stay here as well. I can take Megan and Cade to find Lyle. As soon as we do, we'll all come together here and stay put until morning."

The two women nodded in agreement, so Elle and her partners exited into the hallway, closing the door behind them. As they made their way toward the front stairs, Megan leaned into Elle.

"You didn't mention the circuits or the phone. What gives?" she asked.

"I didn't want to worry them any more than I needed to," she replied. "Lyle missing is bad news enough."

Megan wrung her hands as she walked. "Whatever gets us through this night."

As the trio descended the front staircase, Elle felt a slight breeze. The sound of rain was louder here, and the air smelled faintly of marsh and salt. From the front hall, she could see the large front door to Aldermire was ajar. It swung loosely on massive hinges as the rain showered the interior foyer.

Without being asked, Cade strode through the water puddled across the entrance's stone floor. He looked out into the rain, casting the flashlight's beam in a wide arc for any signs of the missing MacUspaig heir. Finding nothing but more rain, he shut the great door and brushed the water from his shoulders and hair.

"I can't see anything out there," he said. "It's like a wall of water between us and the rest of the world."

"Do you think he actually made it outside?" Megan asked.

Elle shook her head. "I have no clue, and I don't know if taking our chances in the pump house is such a good idea. Let's check the rooms down here, then head back up to the study."

"The basement is all yours," Megan said with a smile.

"Love you, too," Elle replied.

Beyond the foyer, the front rooms revealed no trace of Lyle. Even in the darkness, the formal parlor, rarely used since the death of Hendry's wife, was pristine and antiseptic. The trio moved as a group through the downstairs study and into Stuart's former office. As Elle suspected, the ground floor landline that once occupied a corner on the dead man's desk had gone missing.

"I know we can agree that we're worried about Lyle," Megan said as they checked the study's closets, "but this is starting to get to me. None of this makes any sense. Can we please just go back upstairs and wait until morning with the others?"

"And what if we're wrong?" Elle asked. "Maybe he just got hurt or he needs our help. If I didn't look for him, at the very least, that would be on my head. We've got four or five more rooms, then we'll head up and stay put."

"I think she's right," Cade added. "Mom, nothing is going to happen to you with all three of us here. Let's do one lap down here and then we're out."

Megan sighed, staring at the spot where the office phone once sat. She thought for a moment, then nodded.

"Cade, honey, it's not me I'm worried about," she said. "I'd never forgive myself if something happened to you. Let's make it quick, then we hunker down for the night."

After a half-hearted search of the unused servants' quarters and mudroom in the back of the house, the trio stood at the top of the basement stairs. Whether it was the storm, the night or the absence of ambient light, their combined flashlight beams did nothing to split the darkness of the cavern below.

"Now that we're standing here, I've got to tap out on this one," Megan said, raising her hands in apology. "I've already been down there once tonight, and it doesn't fill me with hope and warm feelings to think about going down there again."

"I have to agree with you," Elle said after some thought. "And even if he is down there, the piles of junk and God only knows what would make it like looking for a needle in a haystack."

As a compromise, they called his name several times; Lyle never responded.

The kitchen turned up nothing of interest, although Elle did manage to secure an apple and two bananas before they moved to the dining room. She gave it a second thought and with her fellow searchers in tow, she returned to the industrial stainless-steel refrigerator to grab a bottle of water.

"Anyone else want one?" she asked.

When Cade raised his hand, Megan was quick to comment. "Don't open that door when the power's out," she snapped. "The food will spoil faster."

Cade and Elle stared at her, speechless. After a moment, Cade laughed and shook his head.

"Yeah, Mom, because our biggest problem tonight is the chance of bad milk," he said with a smirk. "Elle, grab me one of those, will you?"

"Sorry," Megan relented. "Mom reflexes. Elle, can I have one, too?"

Now fully stocked with water and fruit, the trio performed a cursory scan of the dining room then moved into the library. The large chairs and table lamps made a quick search impossible. The last glow of the evening's fire cast distorted shadows around the room in a labyrinth of dark and darker.

Standing a moment at the French doors, Elle looked out to the grand plaza. Even through the rain and darkness, she could just make out the spot where Stuart lay just a few nights ago. She sighed a breath of relief to see the spot empty, almost expecting to see the younger MacUspaig had met a similar fate.

"Mom, Elle, I found him," Cade's voice called softly. Moving past the overstuffed chairs to the fireplace hearth, Elle knew her relief was premature. In front of the dying embers, Lyle MacUspaig lay face down. Despite the darkness of the room, Elle could see the concave distortion in the back of his skull and the pool of blood that now stained the wooden floor. A foot away, a heavy iron club, no more than a foot and a half in length, had been cast to the side.

"Oh, God," Megan muttered, holding her son's shoulder for balance.

While Elle scanned the room for any movement or suspicious shadow, she asked, "Megan, is that the mace that went with the dagger on the study mantle?" From the corner of her eye, Elle saw her nod in agreement.

With an overwhelming sense of déjà vu, she knelt down and checked Lyle for a pulse. Given the depth of the blow to his skull, she wasn't surprised when she found none.

"Okay, that's it," Elle continued. "We are going upstairs to join the others. I can't tell what's happened, but something else is far less likely to happen if we stick together."

"Agreed," Cade answered. His mother just kept nodding.

14

One for sorrow, two for joy,
Three for a girl, four for a boy.
Five for silver, six for gold,
And seven for a secret that must never be told.

— Old Scottish Proverb

The family sat around the dining room table in silence. Hendry had demanded to see his son's body, and the shock had robbed him of his will to walk. While Lainie cried quietly into her hands, Caroline's sobs perforated the quiet of the room.

"And there is no way to reach the police?" Elle asked again.

Cade shook his head. "The only two working phones in the house are missing. And cell phones are useless on Roan. Trust me, I've been over every inch of this island trying to get a signal. The whole thing is one big dead zone."

"What damn good would the police be anyway?" Hendry said, his voice hoarse with grief. "My only son is dead." He pounded his fist against the oak table and cried, "No one is so great that he can avoid the misery that will rise up when he strives against God."

“There may be another way,” Elle noted, ignoring the man’s outbursts. “There’s a landline in the red cottage, maybe one in the white cottage, too.”

“Are you volunteering?” Megan asked.

“If it gets us off this damn island, then yes, I’m volunteering,” she replied.

“I’ll go with you,” Cade added.

“Like hell you will,” his mother answered.

“Mom, I’m not arguing with you on this one. She can’t go alone. This is our best shot. You stay here with the family, and Elle and I can call the police.”

“While you run your damned fool’s errand, I’m going to my study,” Hendry said meekly. Lainie offered to help him out of his chair, but he refused. With great effort, he stood and balanced himself without support. To Elle he looked a full decade older than when she had first arrived at Roan.

Megan thought for a few moments and relented. “Just please, Cade, go straight out and come straight back.”

“We will, I promise,” Elle answered for him. “Why don’t the rest of you go upstairs. Either stick together or lock yourselves in your rooms, I don’t care which at this point.”

“Be safe, honey,” Megan said to her son. To Elle, she leaned in and whispered, “If anything happens to my boy, I will hunt you down and kill you myself.”

From where Elle stood at Aldermire’s back kitchen door, the red cottage was less than 500 feet in a direct line. In the overlapping waves of wind and rain, the darkened guesthouse was all but invisible to her now. Without the caution of an umbrella or raincoat, she and Cade sprinted through the darkness, stepping over fallen branches and scattered patio furniture.

"If we get wet, then we get wet," she had reasoned. "Wet or dry, we'll still be alive."

As they huddled under the small eve in front of the red cottage, Elle tried the door. Three turns and a heavy push confirmed it was locked.

"Damn!" she exclaimed to Cade over the wind. "The keys are on my dresser back at the house."

Without a word, he picked up a small brick from the cottage garden and broke out a small pane of glass just above the knob. Three seconds later, they were inside the guesthouse, water from their clothing collecting in huge puddles on the wooden floor.

"I never would have thought of that," Elle said with a blank expression. "And I had zero interest in running back to Aldermire in this."

"Well, not my usual style," he replied looking down at the broken glass, "but honestly, who's left to care?"

Elle flicked the switch just inside the door, but the lights never responded. She cast her flashlight's beam across the room and into the efficiency kitchen. In three steps she was standing in front of the old slimline telephone that sat on the truncated counter. She held her breath and picked up the receiver.

The dial tone that buzzed in her ear was a thing of beauty. Sensing her relief, Cade exhaled with her. Had the rain not drenched her face, he may have noticed her crying. From memory, she dialed Jonah Tanner's cell phone.

"I'm calling Tanner," she explained. "I don't know if they can get someone here in the storm, but at least I'm certain he'll try."

"You have his number memorized?" Cade asked. "Seriously?"

Elle rolled her eyes in the darkness. "He gave it to me a few years ago," she replied. "It's a long story. It's come in handy every now and then."

As she finished speaking, she heard his voice. "Tanner here," he said in his most official tone.

"Jonah, it's Elle," she replied with haste. "I'm calling you from my cottage on Roan. Lyle MacUspaig has been killed. I don't know who did it, but it was intentional. They also cut power and phones to the house."

"Damn, Elle. Is everyone else okay?"

"As far as I know, yes. Cade and I came out to the cottage to use the phone. Thank God it still works," she answered. "We've got to go back and keep an eye on the others."

"Are you sure that's the best idea?" he asked.

"We're safe for now, but I don't know for how long and from whom. Cade is understandably worried about his mother still stuck in that house, and frankly, I agree that there is safety in numbers."

"Go back and find someplace secure where you and anyone else you trust will be safe until we arrive. I'm looking at the radar now, and it may be another half hour or so before I can get my guys out to the island. Elle, I promise we'll be there as soon as we can. Just hold out 'til then."

"Got it," she replied. "Unless anything changes, we'll be upstairs in either Hendry MacUspaig's study or one of the bedrooms. And please, Jonah, be careful."

She hung up the phone and took a deep breath. "Okay, you heard him. Let's get back to the house and lock ourselves in for the night. Another hour and we should be okay."

"Whatever you say."

As they ran across the lawn for the second time, a series of lights at Aldermire caught Elle's eye. From her position 200 feet from the main house, she could see flashlight beams—perhaps two or three—casting about through the windows on the second floor.

Elle and Cade burst through the back kitchen door, nearly colliding with Megan as she turned the corner from the back stairs.

"Honey, are you alright?" she asked Cade, nearly frantic.

"I'm fine, what's going on?" he replied.

"I was locked in my room with Caroline, and we heard a crash over the sound of the thunder, like something breaking. I called out for Lainie or one of the others, but no one answered. I was so worried about you that I left Caroline sitting there and was going to head to the cottage myself." She paused for a moment. "Did it work? Please tell me the phone worked."

"I just spoke to Jonah," Elle replied. "I told him about Lyle, and he will be here the instant the weather permits." Megan held her chest and took a deep breath.

"So what made the noise?" Cade asked.

"I have no idea," his mother replied. "It sounded like it came from the first floor, but with all the wind and thunder, I could be wrong. Wait, did you all hear that?"

The trio paused and listened.

"What are we listening for?" Cade asked.

As he finished the question, a faint voice came through the dining room. "Hello?" it asked.

Elle led the other two through the back hall and into the front foyer. At the top of the landing, Caroline stood with her flashlight, flanked by Lainie and Hendry on either side.

"Is everyone okay?" she asked with rising fear in her voice.

"We are fine," Elle called up. "The police are coming as soon as they can. Where is Leith?"

Caroline looked at each of the others, then shook her head. "We haven't seen him," she replied. "I think we were each in our rooms when we heard the noise."

Lainie cried out with an odd, anguished squeal. "Oh God, please find him," she begged. She raced down the steps as Caroline followed behind her. Hendry shook his head, then slowly made his way downstairs to where the others waited.

"This time, we'll all search together," Elle said.

Elle and Megan stood at the French doors overlooking the grand terrace. The others sat in the next room, slotted into their familiar spots around the dining room table. Every flash of lightning illuminated the bundle of cloth and limbs that sat motionless just four or five feet outside the doors. While Elle did her best to ignore the body in the library, she tried to make sense of Leith Daleroch's final moments.

"This really is a nightmare," Megan whispered, "a horrible, never-ending nightmare. Did he jump?"

"I doubt it," Elle replied as she pointed to the pile of foliage and rubble beside him. "If he was jumping, why take the planter with him? My guess is that he tried to save himself but without success."

Another bolt of lightning lit the terrace, and Megan had to turn away. From the dining room, both women could hear Lainie crying.

"At this rate, there won't be anyone left by the time the police get here," Megan said in a whisper. "Any suggestions?"

"Exactly what we discussed before. Everyone in their rooms with the doors locked. And this time, no one comes out, no matter what we hear."

"You've got my vote," Megan replied as they moved past Lyle's draped body and into the dining room.

"Everyone, we just have another half hour or so to hold on," Elle said to the remaining family members. "Let's all go upstairs and lock ourselves in wherever we feel safest. Jonah and his team should be here soon."

"Do what you will," Hendry MacUspaig said, rising from his chair. "One way or the other, I'd be happy dying as I lived, surrounded by my history in my study." He paused as he stumbled for balance. "If someone could just help me up," he added with a growl.

Lainie looked around the room with a dull expression. She took a deep breath and stood from her seat.

"I'll take Mr. MacUspaig up to his study," she said without emotion. "Then I suppose I'll be in my room."

"I'll feel safest in my own room," Caroline said softly as she stared at each of the others one at a time with suspicion.

"Elle, if you want to sit with us, Cade and I would be happy for the extra company," Megan offered.

"Let's all go up together," Elle suggested. "Then, everyone just sit tight. It's almost over." She hoped she came across more certain than she felt.

"The notes just don't make any sense," Elle said aloud from her seat on her bedroom floor next to Angus.

"Elle, none of this makes any sense," Megan replied. "Stuart murdered? Okay, I can see that happening. Lyle murdered? A stretch, but it's possible. But Leith murdered? Not damn likely. And who the hell would want to kill all three?"

"Maybe there *is* someone in the house we don't know about," Cade suggested.

"I didn't think so before, but I'm beginning to hope you're right," Elle replied. "Otherwise it's down to Lainie and Caroline, and I don't peg either of them as a killer. Hendry, neither."

"And each of them was with someone else for at least one of the deaths," he noted.

"But my mind keeps coming back to the notes," Elle said. "Why spook Stuart with the fifth commandment if he had nothing to do with Quacey's death?"

"From everything I've ever heard, he was in Richmond that entire night," Megan confirmed. "So how could he be to blame? And why is that enough to want him dead? And who wanted to meet with Lyle? Why all the cloak and dagger? Why not just sit down and talk to him?"

"And why Mr. Daleroch?" Cade added. "What could he have done? And who would do that to Lainie?"

Elle thought for a moment. "I'm actually kind of worried about her," she said. "The last family she had is gone, and she's sitting alone in her room with a vicious killer in the house."

"We can go check on her," Megan offered, "but we're doing it together."

"You read my mind," Elle replied.

The women each retrieved their flashlights, and Cade unlocked the bedroom door. He quietly opened the door leading into the hallway and peered out into the darkness.

"Free of vicious killers," he reported.

The trio made their way down the hall to Lainie's room. The door was closed, and repeated knocks received no answer.

"Oh, hell," Elle muttered. Without asking the others, she tried the knob and the door slowly opened inward. Two simple candelabras lit the interior of the room, one on either side of an ornate antique dresser. Although her bed was made, her nightgown laid out with care and another candle lit her nightstand, Lainie was not to be found.

Megan made her way quietly across the room, checking both the closet and the adjoining bathroom without success. While Cade looked down the hall in either direction with the stronger of the two flashlights, Elle lifted the candle to better inspect the bedside stand.

Next to an electric alarm clock that no longer kept time was a framed photograph of a young woman. She was blond with green eyes and an engaging smile. Her hairstyle and clothing were at least two decades out of date, and the only jewelry she wore was a delicate silver moon pendant around her neck.

"Do you think she's still with Hendry?" Megan asked after searching the private bath.

"Megan, who is this?" Elle asked without answering the other woman's question.

"That's Quacey," Megan replied. "It's the only photo I've ever seen of her. It's sat on that nightstand as long as I've been at Aldermire."

"Damn," Elle exclaimed under breath. "I had the right sinner but the wrong sin."

15

The torture of a bad conscience is the hell of a living soul.

— John Calvin

Without knocking, Elle pushed against the imposing oak door to Hendry's study. To her surprise, the iron handle turned easily, and the door swung inward. Standing in front of the iron MacUspaig crest, Hendry and Lainie were holding two aperitif glasses of dark liquor. The pair regarded Elle dully and without emotion.

"Ah, Miss Mackay," Hendry greeted her in sober tones. "We were just sharing a nightcap. A little something sweet to end this godforsaken night."

Her eyes darted from the raised glasses to the bar counter. "Both of you, wait," Elle warned. "Put the drinks down. Please, listen to me."

At first, neither moved. After a few seconds, Lainie crossed in front of the fireplace and cocooned herself comfortably in an overstuffed chair. She furrowed her brow as she examined her glass, tentatively sniffing the dark purple liquor. As she contemplated her drink, the MacUspaig patriarch shook his head and gently rebuked Elle's warning.

"Elle, I imagine death has had her fill of us tonight," Hendry said. "Don't you think we've earned a bit of sweet oblivion this evening? Between the two of us, we've lost a father, a son and a trusted friend."

"And a sister," Elle added.

Hendry sighed, his head bobbing. "Elle, that's uncalled for. Why open old wounds with ancient history?" he asked. "Why layer tragedy on top of tragedy?"

"Please, just leave us the hell alone," Lainie pleaded through her teeth. She leaned farther back into the great chair and closed her eyes. "The police will be here in the morning. They will sort this all out. I just want to stay here safe with Hendry until then."

"But you're not safe," Elle warned. "Please, both of you just put down your glasses."

Hendry laughed, his eyes showing emotion for the first time since the evening began. "Elle, you'll have us jumping at our own shadows," he said. "I just poured the drinks myself, so I'm sure we are perfectly safe. Nothing more dangerous than a bit of blackberry brandy. Something to calm the nerves."

"Hendry, you know that's not true," Elle chided. "You're hoping death still has one last appointment at Aldermire tonight."

As Lainie looked from her glass to the old man standing across from her, the first hint of doubt crossed her face. In the fire-lit shadows of the plump easy chair, her blond hair looked almost golden. For a fleeting second, Elle saw traces of Quacey in the tired, frightened woman seated before her. The family resemblance was muddled but unmistakable. As though to break Elle's concentration, Lainie bolted upright in the chair and set the aperitif down on the side table.

With a sigh and a cluck of his tongue, Hendry shook his head. "You Dalerochs are all the same—all caution and no adventure," he said. "Fine, my dear, if you don't need it, I do." He lifted Lainie's glass from the side table and downed each nightcap in a single gulp. "A bit sweet," he noted, "but it will settle the soul."

As Hendry retreated to his chair, Megan and Caroline appeared at the door. Cade brought up the rear, keeping a watchful eye on the two women.

"Give me ten minutes," Elle said. "We need a little privacy. Important family business to discuss."

"Are you saying we're not family?" Megan challenged, although a bit meekly.

"Tonight," Elle said, "you'll probably be happy to not have been born a MacUspaig."

Megan's eyes locked with Elle's and she considered the odd request. "You sure you know what you're doing?" she asked.

"Just let us have ten minutes," Elle repeated.

With a shrug and a quick look at the grim trio in front of the fireplace, Megan acquiesced. "Just yell if you need anything, and I truly mean anything." She closed the study door behind her.

For a few seconds, Elle and Hendry looked at each other in silence. Unable to keep quiet, Lainie burst out, "What the hell is going on? Three people—four people—I care about are dead, and you two are playing some bizarre game. I can't take this."

"It's more than tonight," Elle said as she stepped across the room to stand in front of the seated pair. "We have four different murders that have been committed here at Aldermire. The true tragedy is that each one just keeps instigating and feeding the next."

"Four murders? You count Quacey as a victim?" Hendry asked. "I've said it before and I'll say it again, she left of her own free will. Quite a jump to murder victim, don't you think?"

Elle ignored the old man's prodding and turned to Lainie. "Lainie, what was Quacey's favorite piece of jewelry?" she asked.

Without a moment's hesitation, Lainie replied, "Our mother's necklace. It was a part of her. I can't remember ever seeing her without it. Why?"

"A small Celtic moon pendant, cast in silver?" Elle asked.

"Well, yes," Lainie responded. "That's no secret. You can see it in her picture on my nightstand. I don't think I have a photo of Quacey when she wasn't wearing it."

"Did it have a thistle engraved on the back?" Elle continued.

Now Lainie hesitated, her tongue tripping over words. "Yes, but how did you know that?"

"While doing my research on Clan MacUspaig, your father and I spent hours in the newly opened crypt," Elle explained. "Four weeks ago, I found a necklace just like it. It was on the ground in a dark corner near Reverend Padraig MacUspaig's vault. It was clearly out of place, so I picked it up and figured I'd study it later."

"How?" Lainie asked. Her eyes widened, and she covered her mouth with one hand. "Quacey would never, never have left without that necklace."

"Lainie, I don't think Quacey ever left Roan Island," Elle offered gently. "Yes, she disappeared here, but I also think your sister died here. And her death is the spark that set all of this into motion. Every horrible thing we all have experienced this weekend started then and there."

Lainie forced herself farther back into her chair, as though it offered protection from what she was hearing. Her eyes focused and turned to Hendry in supplication. "What is she talking about? We were both here when Quacey left," she said. "Why would anyone kill her? And who?"

Hendry sat still on his throne, his head shaking slightly. He lifted his eyes and turned to Elle. "You know nothing of what you speak," he warned. "Our past is in the past. Only God can judge us for our sins."

Elle replied, "Let's look at this from a more practical perspective, Hendry. When Quacey disappeared, only you, your late wife, Leith and Lainie were at Aldermire."

Hendry didn't respond, but Lainie nodded, appearing desperate to follow Elle's logic.

"When Stuart was killed only Megan, Caroline and I were unaccounted for," she continued. "When Lyle was killed, only Megan and I were together. Finally, when Leith died, the two of you were the only family without clear alibis. If we are looking for a single murderer, this simply can't be right."

Lainie looked lost. "I don't know what this means," she said, shaking her head.

"Lainie, no one person could be responsible for any three or four of the deaths," Elle explained. "Everyone is alibied by at least one other person for one or more of the murders. That leaves only one possible explanation: we have more than one killer, either working together or independently of one another."

Lainie pulled her arms around herself as she thought over Elle's words. "I still don't understand why. Why kill Quacey or the MacUspaigs? Why kill my father?"

"I think I have some of this pieced together," Elle continued. "Earlier this weekend two anonymous notes were found here at Aldermire, one each to Stuart and Lyle. While very similar, each was in slightly different handwriting. Two notes and two very coincidental choices in murder weapons suggest our killers were working in tandem. If we consider that one murderer may be covering for another, that blows just about every alibi out of the water."

"Oh my God," Lainie muttered as her eyes darted up to where the dagger and mace once sat on display. "What notes? I still don't understand what this all means."

"We think that yesterday, Lyle received a note asking for a secret meeting. The night Stuart died, he received a note that was a little more cryptic," Elle continued. "It admonished him for breaking the fifth commandment. At least I'm pretty sure that's what it meant."

Lainie closed her eyes and thought back to her Catholic school training. "Thou shalt not kill?" she asked. "Wait. You said this started with Quacey. What did either of them have to do with her disappearance? Stuart was in Richmond, and Lyle wasn't even born when she left. How could either be accused of killing her? How could either be blamed for breaking that commandment?"

"That tripped me up, too," Elle admitted. "I didn't know why that note was given to Stuart, so there was some piece of the puzzle I was missing. That was until earlier tonight when you, Hendry, gave us your thoughts on a bad conscience, something like 'A bad conscience is hell to a living soul.' That was a quote from John Calvin, wasn't it?"

"Aye," Hendry responded. "You are close. 'The torture of a bad conscience is the hell of a living soul.'"

"I should have recognized Calvin's words. Thinking back, you've quoted him several times this weekend. I spent three years researching the founders of modern Calvinism in Scotland. Hendry, you're a lifelong Calvinist. Am I right?"

"Aye," Hendry repeated, his shoulders slumping ever so slightly. "I suppose there is no running from the eyes of God. 'For there is no one so great or mighty that he can avoid the misery that will rise up against him when he resists and strives against God.'"

Lainie continued to regard Hendry with suspicion and horror. "But what does any of this have to do with Quacey?" she asked.

"We always think of the Ten Commandments as being, well, written in stone," Elle said. "But several Christian churches order them differently. In Calvinism, the fifth commandment, traditionally, is 'Honor thy father and thy mother.' That is the piece I was missing. And that is the sin for which Stuart was killed," she concluded.

"But I thought you said this all started with Quacey's disappearance," Lainie said. "What does that have to do with family honor? You said that 'Thou shalt not kill' makes more sense."

Hendry sat on his throne, head bowed and shaking.

"It does make sense, but not as I had first thought," Elle continued. "And perhaps it made the most sense to your father. Lainie, I know this may be difficult, but we need to talk about Quacey's death, not her disappearance."

Lainie nodded bleakly in quiet agreement.

"Hendry, you've made no bones about the importance of your family name," Elle noted. "When Quacey married your only son, the MacUspaig clan was assured a fertile future. You were so sure that you granted Aldermire to Stuart and his new bride."

"Aye," he acquiesced. "It should have been the MacUspaig home for generations. This house was built with our own hands, and no one else should reap the rewards of our kin's blood and sweat."

"There was one major flaw in your family's longevity," Elle said. "When it appeared that Quacey couldn't or wouldn't bear children, your family name was at risk. Your golden boy was to remain childless, and there was nothing you could do to change his fate. What did you offer Quacey to leave Stuart?"

"More than she was worth," Hendry spat. "She refused to even discuss my future heirs with me. And my only boy would see to the death of the MacUspaig name. He loved her more than he valued centuries of our clan's legacy. She had no idea of the importance of the family she married into."

"When she refused to leave, you took control of the family's future—and took Quacey's life with your own hands," Elle continued. "If my hunch is right, you hid her body in the family crypt. There must be tunnels Leith knew nothing about. That's the only way you could have hidden her in the crypt without opening the front gate. I'm guessing she is still there."

Hendry shook his head and tried to hold his silence. At last he replied, "Aye, when I demanded she leave, she never even asked why. She laughed at me. She said her love for Stuart was worth all of Aldermire and more. I choked the very breath from her words."

"When Leith and I opened the crypt, I found Quacey's necklace and gave it, quite accidentally, to the one person who would understand its significance," Elle said. "Lainie, your father never acknowledged that he recognized the pendant, but he must have quickly pieced together what it meant for your sister's fate. He'd known for several weeks."

"That bastard poisoned my soul," Hendry growled. "He drove a wedge between Stuart and his family. He convinced my own son to banish the MacUspaig name from Aldermire. Leith admitted as much before I killed him."

Lainie let out an audible gasp, but Elle pushed on.

"He did more than that," Elle said. "Once he suspected Quacey's fate, he played Iago to your Othello. He convinced you that your family name was more important than your actual family. Not that you took a great deal of convincing. And why not? You now had a second son to pick up the MacUspaig standard where the first had let it drop."

"I placed our entire legacy in Stuart's hands, and he spat on it," Hendry said. "He failed to honor his father, his mother, his family name. He was my chosen heir, and he would have given it all away to the highest bidder. Leith understood the history and importance of the MacUspaig clan. And he used that against me."

"I'm guessing you both had a hand in Stuart's murder," Elle said.

"It was Leith's idea," Hendry admitted, "as was the damned note. He suggested I give Stuart one last chance by showing how clear his blasphemy was in the eyes of God. Leith was the wicked voice whispering in my ear. I knew it was an affront to God, but it was the only way to save Aldermire and the family's legacy. If the estate could pass on to Lyle, I'd save my clan and my namesake."

"Who actually used the dagger?" Elle asked.

"I confronted Stuart on the patio and tried to reason with him, but he'd have none of it," Hendry said. "He forsook everything I had taught him of our MacUspaig heritage. He laughed when I begged him to reconsider. When I saw that he had chosen his own path, I held his shoulders and Leith did what needed to be done."

"Oh, my God," Lainie repeated.

"It wasn't perfect, and I knew we would likely be caught," he explained. "I don't even pretend to understand the modern police. All I know is that it would have kept Aldermire from being sold. It would have passed on to Lyle and his children for another dozen generations."

"Until Leith's full plan came to fruition," Elle added.

"Aye," Hendry said. "He brought me to my study after the lights had gone out. He said he needed to visit his room, but instead he murdered my last son in cold blood. Lyle was the only one who could carry on the family name. Leith isolated us here during the storm. He lured Lyle to his fate with promises of wealth and the deed to Aldermire. He took my boy's life."

"Your sons' lives for his daughter's life," Elle noted. "An eye for an eye."

"He's doomed the MacUspaigs," Hendry moaned. "We'll vanish from the Earth like so many clans before us. Damn him."

"For you, it's a fate worse than death," Lainie added, suddenly showing life. "You killed my sister, and my father took his revenge. I don't pretend to condone his actions, but Stuart and Lyle paid for your sins. God rest their souls, but you both got what you deserved."

"Aye, Leith got what he deserved," Hendry said. "When Lyle was found dead, I needed to clear my head. I stepped out on the balcony to smoke my pipe, and Leith told me what he had done to my poor boy. He reveled in it. He gloated over my dead sons, cursing my family and my name for taking his Quacey. I sent him right over the edge to his fate. His body may have stopped, but I know his soul kept going straight to hell."

"I know you'll join him there one day," Lainie spat at the old man.

Hendry laughed softly, his movements growing short and erratic. "Sooner than you might think, lassie," he said. He leaned back in his oversized chair and closed his eyes for a moment.

"What was in the drinks?" Elle asked.

"I already told you, a little bramble brandy," Hendry chuckled. "And a healthy dose of nightshade root extract. I told you it would settle the soul. No chance of reaching out for help at this point."

Lainie stared at the glasses on the side table. "Why?" she asked.

"Lainie, you were the loose end," Elle explained. "A Daler-och had ended the MacUspaig line, and Hendry wanted to return the favor."

"I hadn't planned any of this," Hendry said after a few short, shallow breaths. "I hadn't worried about getting away with this, either. I just wanted to preserve my family's historic name. Damn you, Leith."

"Lainie, please go and see if there is any sign of help," Elle requested. "The dose may not have been fatal."

Hendry chuckled softly again. "I'm not an amateur, Miss Mackay," he said between labored breaths. "Lainie, I meant for this to be the end for both of us. I did what I did, and in the end I've chosen the coward's way out. Honestly, I've just been stalling both of you. I don't want to die alone."

Hendry opened his eyes one last time, his pupils dilated even in the warm firelight of the study. As the family crest kept guard in front of the fireplace, the patriarch took one final breath, and the last soul of Clan MacUspaig left the Earth.

16

Vengeance is in my heart, death in my hand,
Blood and revenge are hammering in my head.

— William Shakespeare, *Titus Andronicus*

"What the hell just happened here?" Megan asked. "I'm serious. What the *hell* just happened?"

She stood, once again, by the dining room doors overlooking the grand terrace and the gardens of Aldermire. Elle and Cade sat at the table; the warm breakfast just delivered by Deputy Pace remained untouched between them.

Sausage biscuits were a personal favorite of Elle's, but she found she just didn't have an appetite. As the officer left the room, she quietly fed half a biscuit to Angus beneath the table.

"I can only begin to guess," Elle replied as she recalled the past few hours.

Leveraging a short break in the storm, the police had arrived minutes too late to save Hendry MacUspaig from his chosen fate. Once the rain cleared, the three new bodies were photographed and collected by the medical examiner's team. Witness statements were taken, murder weapons were bagged and reports were filed. Despite the wave of relief, none of the remaining family members slept that night.

By first light, Megan and Cade had packed bags and were making hotel arrangements in Saint Andrews. Lainie had the police take her to Wilmington where she planned to spend a few days with a friend of her deceased mother. Caroline had yet to decide where to spend the coming weeks, but she exclaimed, more than once, that it would never again be Aldermire.

"I knew my time on Roan was coming to an end, but I could never have imagined something like this," Megan muttered. "So many senseless deaths and so many questions without answers."

"Well, I've got one question," Cade interjected. "What about the treasure? And wasn't there a box you were looking for? Didn't those have anything at all to do with what happened?"

"As for the wooden box, Leith was just muddying the waters," Elle replied. "He had already tried getting Lyle alone with the note. And, if you recall, everyone was going to be off island that afternoon. We were all heading out for a movie and dinner. He would have had Lyle and Hendry to himself. It would have been so much simpler to kill Lyle and confront his old friend with no one else on Roan."

"You threw a wrench into that plan," Megan noted.

"True, and when I was talking to Leith, the dead wife's mysterious box wasn't even mentioned until I said I was staying at Aldermire. Leith suggested the attic, then the basement. He had plenty of time to set the trap and wait for me to follow the bait.

"If you all hadn't come back so suddenly, he'd probably have killed Lyle then. And yesterday when Lyle announced he would be leaving at dawn, that forced Leith's hand. He grabbed the phones before dinner, then pulled the circuits after leaving the table. It was risky, but he thought he had nothing left to lose. And as for Caroline, I have no clue where she got the idea of treasure hidden on Roan," Elle concluded. "Even for her that's a stretch."

"So where are you headed?" Megan asked.

"My sister has a free room," Elle replied, "and two four-year-old twin boys. So it's probably not all that free after all. Even so, I could use a little family time right now."

"What's the deal with the dog?" Lana asked as Elle cornered the small oriental rug she brought in from the rental van.

"When Lainie took the boat off Roan Island, she just left him there," Elle replied. "I know he wasn't part of the deal, but I didn't want Angus to end up homeless." Angus heard his name and began to wag his stubby tail. "Plus, it's only temporary until I find my own place."

"Your own place?" Lana said. "Baby girl, how's that gonna work when the grant money runs out?"

Elle shrugged and stretched. "I didn't want to jinx it, but I've got a job interview next Tuesday at one. I don't want to say anything more, and it's not exactly in my field, but it's a start."

Lana gave her little sister a wide, generous smile. "Fingers crossed for you, Ellie. You know that Sophie and I would love having you here as long as you need to stay," she continued. "There's no expiration date on that. The dog too."

"You guys are awesome," Elle said with a grin. "And as much as I complain about Mama, I am perfectly happy being a part of this family."

"Please, Ellie, you know she's just horrible because she cares," Lana replied. "Being overbearing and demanding and interfering and...did I leave anything out?"

"Um, controlling and meddling and high-handed," Elle suggested.

"Those, too. That's just her way of showing love. Trust me, baby girl, for a family you could do much worse."

"Lana, you have no idea."

Epilogue

Lunch went far better than Elle had hoped. Megan was in good spirits, and the comradery that had begun late on Roan was beginning to feel like a friendship.

She continued down Market Street to the waterfront and turned to walk past Alton Lennon Federal. On her right huddled a small, unassuming stone building. It was well-appointed but nondescript, the expensive fleet of cars parked in its small lot were the only indicator of life within.

A green wood-and-brass door tucked well back into the brick façade ushered her into a small reception area where a young man with a headset was expertly juggling several calls in three languages. Elle heard English right away and what she thought were snippets of Portuguese and Czech. As she entered, he pointed to a burgundy velvet chair next to a table littered with news and financial magazines. His multiple conversations continued uninterrupted.

After a few moments, an elevator door to the young man's left opened silently, and he again pointed Elle in the general direction. She rose, waved and stepped into the small, buttonless vintage elevator car. Four seconds and what she estimated to be five stories later, the doors again opened, revealing a tastefully decorated office that spanned the entire length of the floor.

Centered in the room stood an antique oak desk faced by a pair of leather guest chairs. Dr. Coira MacLain Buchanan-Berman rose from her desk and greeted Elle with a warm handshake.

"Elle, dear, how kind of you to come," she said. "Considering the week you've had, I wouldn't blame you for disappearing until Christmas."

"I've been happy just spending time away from Roan," she replied.

"I know we are both busy people, so let me tell you a little about Buchanan, Gambrell, Howard & Berman," Coira said, sizing up Elle with her eyes. "We are, for lack of a more specific term, a research firm. We study and attempt to predict human behavior based on demographic, psychographic and historical trends. We work for market research companies, campaign managers, jury selection experts, law firms and anyone else who wants to use society's present and past to predict the future."

Elle cocked her head. "So where do I fit in?"

"I'll cut to the chase. I've spoken at length to Detective Tanner, and I'm impressed by how you handled yourself at Aldermire. That was an unimaginable horror, and you kept you head even when others didn't. And to be honest, I've been reading over your body of published works this week. You have an analytical eye for the intersection of human history and human behavior."

"I appreciate the compliments," Elle admitted.

"They are well deserved, Elle," she continued. "I'd like to offer you a position with our historical research team. I'll be the first to admit it, the team is small. We are still determining the best methods to leverage what they can tell us into what we can divine for our clients. The work would be part time, but it would pay handsomely. I'd imagine an ambitious researcher with something to prove to herself would enjoy this type of challenge while still having free time to pursue her own interests."

"You know, I think she might," Elle replied.

"I know this is sudden, but do you have any questions about the job?" Coira asked.

Elle thought for a few moments. "Nothing comes to mind, but I'm sure I'll think of something as soon as I leave."

Coira laughed. "It's human nature. I'll have a complete job prospectus and offer delivered to your sister's house on Eagle Island. Do you have any questions that aren't about the job?"

Elle thought again. "While I was at Aldermire, Caroline mentioned something about a treasure. It sounds ridiculous, but I've been wondering if there was any truth to it. Do you have any idea where she may have heard such a thing?"

"Well, from me," Coira admitted. "When Carrie was much younger, she would accompany me to Roan while I met with Hendry and Stuart regarding the house or the estate. Mind you, this was almost twenty years ago. She has always been a handful and in need of constant attention. So I told her a tale of a fantastic treasure buried somewhere on the island. It would keep her busy for hours."

"That explains quite a bit."

"There's something else you may want to know about Roan," Coira said in a more somber tone. "I spoke to Detective Tanner yesterday, and they found Quacey's remains. Her body was sealed in an unmarked niche in the MacUspaig crypt. The coroner noted that her hyoid bone was broken in several places, suggesting she was strangled."

Elle shook her head and muttered, "Two lovers doomed to never find one another at Aldermire; it's like history repeating itself."

"One last thing," Coira said as she looked out the bank of windows. "In her coat pocket was a stash of bills, letters and a card she never had the chance to post. The card was addressed to Stuart's hotel in Richmond—she wanted to surprise him with the news that she was pregnant."

ABOUT THE AUTHOR

A lifelong marketing executive, Liam Ashe is a novice novelist with a love for the great authors and sleuths of detective fiction's Golden Age. Growing up on the twisty tales of Agatha Christie, Ngaio Marsh, John Dickson Carr, Ellery Queen and other mystery masters, he marveled at the authors' devious minds and impossible crimes.

Liam's inaugural series, featuring professional researcher and Scottish historian Elle Cunningham Mackay, is an homage to these masters—with a little modern sensibility mixed in. Elle's Scottish-flavored mysteries will immerse the reader in a world of kilts, bagpipes, Highland games and haggis.

Liam's other works include the Arca Noctis series of thrillers starring curiosity store owner Emery Vaughn and a pair of Golden Age series featuring former spy Mafalda Marchand and village vicar James Valentine.

Love classic mysteries? Visit www.liamashe.com and sign up for Liam's free, quarterly email newsletter. You'll receive updates about Elle's newest titles and special ebook offers on his latest mystery and thriller series.